HARLEQUIN
Presents

What can you expect in Harlequin Presents books?

Passionate relationships

Revenge and redemption

Emotional intensity

Seduction

Escapist, glamorous settings from around the world

New stories every month

The most handsome and successful heroes

Scores of internationally bestselling writers

Find all this in our March books—on sale now!

Legally wed,
but he's never said,
"I love you."
They're...

The series where marriages are made
in haste...and love comes later.

Look out for more WEDLOCKED!
wedding stories available only from
Harlequin Presents®.

Diana Hamilton

THE KOUVARIS MARRIAGE

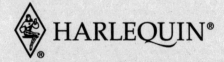

TORONTO • NEW YORK • LONDON
AMSTERDAM • PARIS • SYDNEY • HAMBURG
STOCKHOLM • ATHENS • TOKYO • MILAN • MADRID
PRAGUE • WARSAW • BUDAPEST • AUCKLAND

ISBN-13: 978-0-373-12614-9
ISBN-10:   0-373-12614-X

THE KOUVARIS MARRIAGE

First North American Publication 2007.

Copyright © 2006 by Diana Hamilton.

This edition published by arrangement with Harlequin Books S.A.

® and TM are trademarks of the publisher. Trademarks indicated with
® are registered in the United States Patent and Trademark Office, the
Canadian Trade Marks Office and in other countries.

www.eHarlequin.com

Printed in U.S.A.

PROLOGUE

DONE!

Maddie Ryan straightened, hot and sweaty beneath the sun that blazed from a cerulean sky, and rested her grubby hands on her curvy hips. Every leaf and bloom was perfect, the terracotta planters were arranged in attractive groupings around the arcaded courtyard. The ancient central stone fountain was beautifully restored and finally working, sending a silvery plume of water dancing skywards, then falling back into the shallow stone basin, creating lovely water music.

Everything was ready for tonight's party and her first important commission as a landscape gardener was successfully completed, a commission given by her best friend since schooldays, Amanda.

Thinking of Amanda, she grinned. It was an unlikely friendship—everyone had said so—the tomboy and the fastidious, delicate blonde beauty. But it had worked. On leaving school, Amanda had made her mark as a top model and led a truly glamorous lifestyle. But Maddie, working her way through horticultural college, hadn't been envious, just happy for her—especially when she'd fallen in love and married a fabulously wealthy Greek tycoon.

Then, three months after the wedding, she'd phoned one chilly spring day. 'How do you like the idea of a well-paid working holiday? Cristos has bought this fabulous villa just outside Athens. The house is perfect but the grounds are a neglected mess—especially the courtyard. I fancy something Moorish. Could you take the commission? Cristos said money no object.' A breathy giggle. 'He'd do anything to please me. He's not like your normal Greek male; he treats women as if they have minds of their own!'

Tomorrow Maddie would be returning to England with a fat cheque, a tan, and a bunch of happy memories—and the hope that her mother had fielded at least a couple of responses to her adverts in the local press while she'd been away.

Turning to make one final check on the discreetly hidden irrigation system that kept the planters watered, she noticed the stout wooden door that led from the courtyard to the lemon grove swing open. Thrusting out her lower lip, she huffed away the strands of caramel curls that were tangling with the thick upsweep of her lashes and got an unimpeded view of the hunk—no other description fitted—who had sauntered into the courtyard.

Like her, he was dressed casually. Almost threadbare faded jeans, against her skimpy cotton shorts, and an ancient black vest top that except for size matched her own. One of the locals, she deduced as he strolled towards her, looking for casual work. But, unlike the late adolescents she'd hired to help with the heavy stuff, this guy looked older—thirty-four or -five at a guess.

Out of work, with a wife and a brood of young children? Looking to pick up a few days' pay? What a waste. With looks like his he would never want for work as a male model: tall, dark and gorgeous, his face crafted to guarantee weak knees in the female population. Strong bones, a firm, commanding mouth with just the right hint of sensuality, she listed to herself. Adding, as he came nearer, an intriguing pair of warm golden eyes fringed with sinfully long dark lashes.

Those fascinating eyes held a question as he halted in front of her, and Maddie had to swallow an annoying constriction in her throat as she apologised with genuine sincerity. 'The project's finished. We're no longer hiring. I'm sorry.'

'Is that so?' He didn't look disappointed. He actually smiled. And the effect was electrifying. Fresh perspiration broke out on her short upper lip. A dark eyebrow quirked. 'And you are?'

'Mad.' Qualifying that quickly, in case he thought she really was, she went on, 'Maddie Ryan. Project designer.' Christened Madeleine because her mother, having given birth to three boisterous boys, had longed for a daughter she could dress in pretty clothes and bring up to be ultra-feminine. But Madeleine had refused to answer to anything but Mad—or Maddie, at a pinch—and could clearly remember back to the age of three or four, when her poor mother had tried to dress her in something pink and frilly for her birthday party. She had gone stiff as a board, screaming her head off as she'd refused to wear anything so girly.

She adored her parents, but she idolised her big brothers, and had always set out to prove she could do anything they could do—from climbing the tallest trees and tickling trout to paddling a home-made raft across the lake on the estate where her dad was employed as head groundsman. Eventually her mother had resigned herself to having a tomboy daughter—freckle-faced, permanently grubby, sticking plasters adorning her coltish legs, untameable curls—and loved her more than she'd thought possible.

'So you are English?' The sexy golden eyes wandered over her, and, nodding the affirmative, Maddie felt her flesh quiver as his eyes swept back up to fuse with hers. In all of her twenty-two years no man had ever had this effect on her, and the unaccustomed and scary stinging sensation of intimacy shook her rigid. 'Do you speak my language?' he asked, on a throaty purr that sent something hot sizzling through her veins. Then his eyes dropped to her wide mouth, lips parted as she puzzled over why he should ask that. His attractively accented voice had implied more than mere politeness. 'I am interested to know how you relayed your wishes to your workers.'

'Oh—that!' Maddie relaxed. Friendly question. Friendly she could handle, no problem. She'd had plenty of male friends, both at school and at college. Been best mates with most of the village boys. But never a serious boyfriend. None of her male friends had ever picked her as his special girl. They'd treated her as one of them—come to her with any problems, discussed stuff—but when it came to romance they'd picked the sort of flirty girlies who could simper and giggle for England.

Speedwell-blue eyes smiled. 'No, I don't speak Greek. I picked up a few words from the casuals—' her smile broadened to a wide grin, her neat freckle-banded nose wrinkling '—but I sort of guessed they're not words one would use in polite company! Nikos—the permanent gardener Cristos hired—is pretty fluent in English, and he translated for me.'

Her voice tailed off. Flustered, she noted that he didn't seem to be listening to her side of this strange conversation. Had he simply asked the first thing to come into his too-handsome head just to keep her talking? Because he was back to making that slow, thoroughly unsettling inventory of her too-bountiful body again, his eyes lingering too long for her comfort on the smooth golden thighs directly beneath the ragged hem of her skimpy shorts.

Pressing her knees close together, to guard against a decidedly perverse instinct to shift them apart and tilt her hips towards that gorgeous, power-packed rangy body, she decided to get rid of him. Aiming for repressive, her words emerged in a husky tone she didn't recognise as her own. 'Did you want something? Can I help you?'

Worryingly, he moved just that little bit closer. His broad shoulders lifted infinitesimally, the bronzed skin gleaming like oiled silk, as it made her wonder what that skin would feel like beneath her fingers.

He gave no answer, but the silence sizzled with something unspoken and his slow smile made her tremble, made her wonder what was happening here—because as sure as hens laid eggs no male had ever made her feel this strange before. This—this what? Expectant?

She swallowed thickly just as he said, 'I think that for now you should find shade.' With lazy grace, the lightest of touches, he brushed a strand of damp hair away from her hot forehead. 'You are hot. Very hot!' Golden eyes danced. 'I'll see you around.'

Not if I see you first, was Maddie's wild unspoken thought as she took the hint and scurried away from his unsettling presence, heading for the wide door that led to the cool interior of the villa. Her skin was still tingling where he had so lightly touched it, sending responsive quivers down her spine.

Typical Greek male, she fumed. Most of the casuals had been the same. Unable to stop strutting their stuff when a female was around. She'd been able to overlook them, no trouble at all. She didn't *do* flirting. Didn't know how. Didn't want to know how. Hadn't had any practice.

But the stranger had been different. And how! It had made her feel uncomfortable. An extra large dose of charisma, she decided as she reached the sanctuary of the suite of rooms she'd been given. A knock-out dose that would make him irresistible if he had seduction in mind.

Seduction? She wasn't going to go there. No way! No doubt he acted that way with any female under ninety. So snap out of it, she scolded herself.

Getting out of her work clothes, she headed for the shower and put him quite brutally out of her mind. Or tried to. With little success, she conceded with vast annoyance.

The party was going with the sort of discreet swing that only serious money could contrive. Ultra-glamorous guests wandered out from the lavish buffet to the court-yard, wine glasses elegantly in hand, murmuring con-gratulations for the romance of the strategically placed uplighters, the plants Maddie had chosen for their perfume, the pale roses and sweetly scented jasmine festooning the pillars of the arcade. And because Amanda and Cristos, bless them, had made sure everyone present knew *she* was the creator of the lush loveliness, Maddie kept her fingers crossed that some of the guests might remember her if they needed any work done in the future.

Amanda joined her on the secluded stone seat Maddie had retired to to get her breath back after answering so many horticultural questions, a glass of chilled white wine in her hot hands.

'It's going perfectly. Everyone's impressed. You never know—you might get one or two commissions.'

'I hope so!' Maddie grinned at her friend. 'I'd love to work here again—I've fallen in love with the country! And I'll never be able to thank you enough for thinking of me.'

'Who else would I think of, dolt?' Amanda's lovely face dimpled with affection. 'And take my advice—if you *are* offered a commission, charge top dollar. These people come from the top layer of Greek society— money coming out of their ears—they *expect* to pay mega-bucks. Offer them cut price and they'll come all over squeamish and run a mile!'

'I'll remember that slice of cynicism!' Maddie took a grateful long sip of wine and pushed her untidy fringe out of her eyes with her free hand, her dancing blue eyes wandering between the groups of beautiful people who were slowly circulating, chatting, the women discreetly pricing and placing each other's jewels and designer dresses.

Dressing for the party, Maddie hadn't even tried to compete. Heck, how could she? Willowy she wasn't, and her wardrobe was as sparse as the hairs on a balding man's head. So she'd got into the only dress she'd brought with her—a simple blue shirtwaister, plain but presentable.

She immediately wished she didn't look so ordinary when she saw him.

An uncontrollable something made her heart leap and her stomach perform a weird loop. The guy she'd tagged as a casual worker—magnetic in a white tuxedo, urbane, elegant—was obviously one of the super-wealthy beings her friend mixed with now she'd married into the highest stratum of Greek society. All his attention was being given to the dark, fashionably skinny beauty clinging to his arm as if she'd been grafted there.

'Oops—latecomer. I'd better do my hostess thing.'

Amanda, noticing the unmissable, rose to her feet, and Maddie, because she couldn't help it, asked, 'Who is he?'

'He's gorgeous, isn't he?' Amanda smoothed the ice-blue silk of her skirt and giggled. 'Dimitri Kouvaris—the shipping magnate and a near neighbour. He walked over this morning to discuss a business deal with Cristos—but he's taken! The clinging vine is Irini—some distant family connection, I believe—and the general consensus is that wedding bells are soon to be tolled! So you have been warned!'

Great! Maddie thought bracingly. And the warning was unnecessary. Seeing him in this exalted milieu provided the metaphorical bucket of cold water she'd needed—because despite all her good intentions she hadn't been able to get him or his final words out of her mind. Or the way he'd looked at her, the sexual interest demonstrated by his body language—and what a body!

She had to put a stop to the unwanted and repeated invasion of the totally stupid thought that he might be the one man capable of making her break her vow of chastity. A vow made to herself because her burgeon-

ing career meant far more to her than any romantic en-
tanglement, and because of her need to prove herself to
her parent, who seemed to think that a woman needed
a man to look after her, to make her whole.

Codswallop!—as she'd inelegantly informed her
mother when she'd aired that outdated view.

But she couldn't help watching the latecomers and
noting the way that the hand that wasn't around the
beautiful Irini's waist lifted in a salute of recognition as
he glanced beyond Amanda to where she was sitting on
her stone bench.

Her face flaming, Maddie refused to respond, and
tried to wriggle further back into the shadows. The last
thing she wanted or needed was for him to saunter over,
clinging vine in tow, and humiliate her by reminding her
how she had mistaken him for a casual worker.

If that had been his intention she was spared, when
a group of guests headed by Cristos joined him. But she
squirmed with embarrassment and uncomfortably
strong frissons of something else entirely when his eyes
kept seeking her out. Narrowed, speculative eyes.

A huge shudder racked its way through her. Enough!
She wasn't going to sit here like a transfixed rabbit
while that man stared at her! Clumsily, she shot to her
feet, and headed briskly back to the villa, where his
eyes couldn't follow her, making for her room and the
calming, sensible task of packing for her departure back
to England in the morning.

It was beginning to grow dark when Maddie parked her
old van at the side of the stone cottage that had been her
home for all her life. It had been a tight squeeze with

four children, but her mother had made it a comfy home. Too comfy, perhaps, she reflected wryly. Only Adam, the eldest, had moved out, when he'd married two years ago. He and Anne had been lucky to get a council house on an estate a mile away, his job as a forestry worker providing for his wife and the next generation of Ryans— a toddler of eighteen months and twins on the way.

Sam and Ben still lived at home. Their joint market garden business—supplying organic produce to local pubs and hotels—didn't make enough profit to allow them to move out. Not that they seemed in any hurry to turn their backs on their Mum's home cooking and laundry service.

Taking the key from the ignition she huffed out a sigh. At nearly twenty-three she should be leaving the nest, giving Mum a break. And she would—as soon as her business took off.

The profits from the Greek job were earmarked for new tools, a possible van upgrade and wider advertising—because the local press had only brought in one enquiry for the make-over of a small back garden in the nearby market town. The clients, recently moved in, wanted the usual. What they called an 'outdoor room', with a play area for a young child, the ubiquitous decking and a tiny lawn. Bog standard stuff which she'd completed in five days, and nothing else on the horizon.

Normally optimistic—a bit too Micawberish her dad sometimes said, but fondly—Maddie felt unusually down as she locked the van and headed for the side door that led directly into the warm heart of the house— the kitchen. Mum would be beavering away, preparing the evening meal for when her ravenously hungry menfolk returned. Friday night, she usually made a huge steak pie. Maddie would prepare the massive amount of vegetables as soon as she'd got out of her muddy work boots and shed her ancient waxed jacket.

Fixing a bright smile on her generous mouth—dear old Mum had better things to do than look at a long face—Maddie pushed open the door and her smile went. Her mouth dropped open and her heart jumped to her throat, leaving her feeling weirdly lightheaded.

He was there. Dimitri Kouvaris. In the outrageously gorgeous, impeccably suited flesh. Sitting at the enormous kitchen table, drinking tea, and being plied with shortbread by her pink-cheeked chattering parent.

He looked up.

And smiled.

It was a perfect spring day. The day after his bombshell arrival on the scene. Her blue eyes narrowed, Maddie watched him saunter ahead along the narrow woodland path.

Dressed this morning in stone-coloured jeans that clipped his narrow male hips and long legs, and a casual honey-toned shirt that clung to the intimidating width of his shoulders, he dominated the surroundings. The sea of bluebells, now in promising bud, didn't even merit a glance. She had eyes only for him. And deplored it.

Last night, at Mum's invitation, he'd stayed for supper, integrating easily with her family. He had explained that he'd met her in Athens through a mutual friend, and that as he was in the area on business he'd decided to look her up.

And she might, if she'd tried hard, have believed it.

But not after the way he'd turned up this morning. All bright-eyed and bushy-tailed, smoothly imparting that as he had a free day and Maddie, as he'd discovered— prised out of someone, more likely!—had no work on, he'd appreciate it if she showed him some of the surrounding countryside. He had tossed in the invitation that they all dine with him that evening at his hotel, erasing Mum's tiny questioning frown at a stroke.

But Maddie was still questioning.

Why should a drop-dead handsome, rotten rich Greek tycoon with a gorgeous fiancée take the trouble to 'look up' an ordinary working girl and her ordinary family? A stranger to male sexual interest, she wasn't so green as to fail to recognise it when it came her way. She'd registered it on that first day back in Athens. She chewed worriedly on her full lower lip. Trouble was, it was mutual, and she was drawn to him when common sense dictated that she should be running a mile.

Turning as the narrow path debouched onto a wide grassy meadow, Dimitri waited for her, his heartbeats quickening. Glossy curls surrounded her flushed heart-shaped face, her sultry lips were parted; her lush body was clothed in faded jeans and a workmanlike shirt. She was as unlike the elegant designer-clad females who threw themselves at him on a tediously regular basis as it was possible to be.

Testosterone pumped through his body. Self-admittedly cynical about the female half of the population, who looked at him and saw nothing but spectacular wealth, this immediate and ravaging physical awareness had never happened to him before. And no way was he about to knock it. He wanted her and would have her—would fight to the death to claim her!

'Why are you here? What do you want?' She sounded breathless. She *was* breathless. Yet the pace he'd set hadn't been in the least taxing. All part and parcel of the effect he had on her, she conceded uneasily, and quivered as he took her hand and raised it to his lips.

The warmth, the firmness of his mouth as it trailed over the backs of her fingers, took what was left of her breath away. And when he murmured, 'You want the truth?' it took an enormous effort of will to look him in the eyes.

'What else?' she said.

Meeting those spectacular, mesmeric golden eyes had been a big mistake, she registered, as her knees went weak and simultaneously her breasts peaked and thrust with greedy urgency against the thin cotton of her shirt.

As if he knew exactly what was happening to her, his long strong hands went to her waist, easing her against his body, making her burningly, bone-crunchingly aware of the hard extent of his arousal.

Feverishly torn between what her mind was telling her and what her body craved, it took some moments before she registered his, 'I need to get back to Athens within the month. And when I go I will take you with me. As my wife.' When it did, her mind took over with a vengeance.

Pulling away from him, she squawked, 'Have you gone crazy? How can you want to marry me? It's madness. You hardly know me!' Then her eyes narrowed to scornful slits. 'Is that the way you usually get into a girl's knickers? Promise to marry her?'

Shaken by his sudden peal of laughter, she could

only splutter as he folded his arms around her and vowed, 'I knew I wanted you in my body and in my soul the first time I saw you. And if that is crazy, then I like being crazy. Tonight, at dinner, I will ask your father's permission to court you. And then I will do everything in my power to persuade you to accept me.'

At her shaky accusation, 'You *are* mad!' he lowered his head and kissed her. And all the niggling questions as to why a guy like him, who could pick and choose between the world's most beautiful women, should earmark *her* as his future bride disappeared for the next earth-shattering couple of hours.

CHAPTER ONE

His face like thunder, Dimitri Kouvaris strode down the first-storey corridor of his sumptuous villa on the outskirts of Athens, hands fisted at his sides, his wide shoulders as rigid as an enraged bull about to charge.

Eleni, the youngest member of his household staff, flattened herself against the wall at his approach, and only expelled her pent-up breath as he shot down the sweeping staircase two treads at a time.

The soles of his handmade shoes ringing against the marble slabs, he crossed the wide hallway and after a cursory rap entered his aunt's quarters.

'Did you know about this?' he demanded on a terse bite, lobbing over the piece of paper crumpled into his fist. And he watched, the gold of his eyes dark with inner fury, as the thin pale fingers of his father's elder spinster sister smoothed the creases out.

The few words burned like acid into his brain.

Our marriage is over. My solicitor will be in touch regarding our divorce.

Three months and she said it was over! No explanation. Nothing but a note left on the pillow of their opulent marriage bed. How dared she?

'She dishonours the Kouvaris name!' he bit out, and the silvery head rose from her prinked-lipped perusal. The sharp black eyes were disdainful as his seventy-year-old aunt dropped the note on the small table at her side and fastidiously wiped her fingers on a silk handkerchief.

'You dishonoured our family name when you made her your bride,' Alexandra Kouvaris pronounced, with a profound lack of compassion. 'A common gold-digger with her eye obviously on a handsome divorce settlement. A high price to pay for an abortive attempt to get an heir, nephew.' She settled back in her chair with a rustle of black silk and reached for the book she'd been reading, dismissing him. 'No, I didn't know she'd gone. I am not in her confidence and I have not pined to be in that position. I suggest you check the contents of your safe to see how much of the jewellery she persuaded you to lavish on her she's taken with her.'

His mouth flat with distaste, Dimitri swung on his heels and left. He couldn't verbally flay his aunt for voicing what everyone would be thinking—although he'd had to bite his tongue to stop himself from doing just that. In the mood he was in he'd lash out at anyone who dared to breathe in his presence, he conceded savagely. In scant seconds he was back in the bedroom he'd shared with his bride, dragging open hanging cupboards and drawers, eventually standing, brows clenched, staring out of one of the tall windows that gave a partial view of the distant Acropolis.

She seemed to have left in just the clothes she was

wearing, her passport and handbag her only luggage. Not one item of designer clothing or jewellery was missing. Was she, as his aunt had stated, going for the much larger prize? Aiming to reach a divorce settlement of half of his vast wealth, making him a laughing stock?

His strong teeth ground together. Over his dead body! Prick a Greek male's pride and the wrath of the gods would descend in dire retribution!

Hadn't he given her everything a woman could possibly want? An enviably beautiful home, unlimited funds, servants to cater to her every whim, great sex. His tight features turned dark with temper as too-vivid memories of the way his pre-marriage largely ignored lunch-breaks had turned into sheer paradise between the sheets with his wife, because the hours before night-time had always seemed impossible to get through without availing himself of the delights of her luscious, responsive body.

Had her generous response been nothing but an act? His lovemaking something to be endured to keep him sweet and unsuspecting until she sneaked away and petitioned for divorce?

No one did that to Dimitri Kouvaris! *No one!*

Turning in driven haste, he used his mobile to instruct his senior PA to cancel all meetings for the next three days. He stuffed a few necessities into an overnight bag with his free hand. Then, ending the call, he keyed in the number of the airport and finally, on receiving the information he needed, contacted the pilot of his private jet.

Tears welled in Joan Ryan's tired eyes as she turned to slide the kettle onto the hotplate of the ancient Aga. That dratted inner shaking had started up again, and over the last twenty-four hours she had drunk enough tea to float a battleship.

Nevertheless, she had to be sympathetic and helpful, put her other problems aside, because no sooner had Joe, her husband—who should by rights be resting, according to doctor's orders, following his heart scare, not getting himself stressed out—together with their three sons walked out of the door than her son-in-law had walked in. And dropped another whopping bombshell.

Maddie had walked out on their marriage.

Maddie wanted a divorce.

It couldn't be happening, she thought on a spurt of uncomprehending agitation. She couldn't for the life of her understand how that marriage had gone so wrong, so quickly. Her daughter had looked radiant with happiness when she'd made her wedding vows in the small parish church just three months ago. She and Joe had been so happy too. Just fancy—their tomboy daughter, who'd never even had a proper boyfriend, marrying such a handsome, wealthy, generous dream of a man. Their adored Maddie stepping ecstatically into an assured future.

And now this!

Dimitri looked strained—as any man would after such a shock, not to mention a headlong dash from Greece and driving up here in a hired car. So a nice cup of tea…

She turned, carried the pot to the big old table, and noted that he had sat himself in Joe's chair, his finely made yet strong hands clenched on the pitted pine tabletop.

'I wish I could help,' Joan mourned, feeling useless. 'For the life of me, I can't understand it. She's never given the smallest hint that anything was wrong in her phone calls. But then, she wouldn't.' She dredged up a sigh. 'That's Maddie for you. She's always had a streak of independence a mile wide.' Hand shaking, she covered the pot with its padded cosy. 'I've heard nothing since her last call a week ago. She hasn't turned up here.'

With an effort, Dimitri forced his hands to relax, flatten against the grainy surface. Joan Ryan was obviously as much at sea as he was.

Forget the acid burn of anger inside him. Clearly the poor woman was worried sick. He liked Maddie's parents—admired their capacity for hard work, their honesty, their love for their family. He couldn't bring himself to tell Joan that her beloved daughter was a sly, scheming gold-digger, marrying him only for what she'd decided she could screw out of him!

He wouldn't have believed it himself until today. Women had been coming on to him since he'd hit his late teens, and he'd learned to suss out gold-diggers from a hundred paces. He would have staked his life on Maddie being genuine, wanting him only for himself, wanting children as much as he did. Had his brain gone soft that first time he'd seen her, wanted her as he'd never wanted any other woman, his heart and soul telling him that here was the one woman in the world he could trust implicitly?

But what other explanation could there be? Colour scorched across his angular cheekbones. Until today their marriage had been fantastic. Not a cross word, just soft words and smiles. Laughter, joy. She'd been just that little bit quieter of late, he'd noted, and once, when he'd gently asked if there was anything wrong, she'd turned that lovely smile on him, reached for him, and assured him that everything was perfect.

An obvious and utterly devious truth—because everything had been going to her greedy plan. He truly didn't want to believe that of her—not of her. But, lacking any other explanation, he had to face it.

Joan pulled out a chair, sat heavily, and poured the tea with a shaking hand. Compassion for her distressed state forced him to say, 'Try not to worry. She'll turn up. She would have taken a scheduled commercial flight, so it would take her much longer to get to Heathrow and then make her way here than it took me. Where else would she go?' He'd checked the departure times of flights to the UK, guessing she would be heading for home. 'Can you think of anywhere else?'

Unable to speak for the lump in her throat, Joan shook her head. The lump assumed monumental proportions as Dimitri supplied reassuringly, 'She'll turn up here. I'm sure of it. But should she phone ahead I must ask you not to tell her I'm here. I need to talk to her, to sort things out.'

Carefully, keeping his tone gentle, schooling out the anger, the outraged pride of the Greek male, he covered her workworn hand with his own—because Joan Ryan was a patently good woman, and none of this was her fault. 'You mustn't worry.'

Kindness was her undoing. She'd genuinely had no intention of burdening him with her family's problems—certainly not while he was so upset over Maddie's desertion. But Joan couldn't stop the torrent of sobs that racked her comfortable frame, and then her handsome, caring son-in-law fetched the box of tissues

from the windowsill, slid it in front of her and put a compassionate hand on her shoulder.

'What's wrong, Joan?' he asked. He'd expected her
to be puzzled and upset by her daughter's behaviour, but
not to the extent of breaking down entirely. 'Tell me. I
might be able to help.'

It all came pouring out.

It was late, and as dark as a country night could be. The
taxi driver was grumbling under his breath as he nego-
tiated the twisting, narrow, tree-hung lanes. Maddie,
leaning forward, had to give him directions.

'It's about a mile ahead,' she told him as he took the
left-hand fork she'd just indicated. 'I'll tell you when
we get there.' She subsided, stuck with her own
thoughts. And they weren't pleasant company.

The journey from Athens had been a complete
nightmare. She wasn't going to think about her
broken marriage—it hurt too much—so she'd think
about the trials of her flight to freedom instead. Her
departure from Athens had been delayed by a couple
of hours. Eventually reaching Heathrow, she'd queued
for ages to get her euros changed to sterling, then
headed for Euston and sat over a cup of what was
supposed to be coffee while she'd waited for a train
to Shrewsbury. She had phoned home to say she'd be
arriving—probably at midnight at this rate, after the
difficulty of finding a driver willing to take her way
out to the sticks.

Mum had sounded a bit odd on the phone. Maddie
hadn't told her that her marriage was over—that would
have to be done face to face. It would upset her

parents; she knew that. They thought she'd made the perfect marriage.

And it could have been so perfect. She'd loved him so very much. Enough to push her doubts as to why he should want to marry so far beneath him out of her mind. Doubts that had trickled slowly but inexorably back on her return to Athens as his bride. Her insides twisted painfully, and she had to stiffen her spine and remind herself that she would not be used. That she would never regret walking out on him, that she would not weep for him.

Did he think she was without pride? Did he think that she was too stupid to discover the truth? That she was too besotted with him, too enthralled by his magnificent body, his lovemaking, the things he could give her, ever to go looking for it?

As the headlights picked out the driveway to the small stone house she rocketed thankfully out of her pointless mental maunderings and stated, with feeling, 'You can drop me here.'

Tears of weak relief blurred her eyes. Home at long last! To the beginning of a new and independent life. Apart from starting divorce proceedings, she need never allow a single thought centring on Dimitri Kouvaris into her head again.

Stumbling with fatigue, she headed up the short track after paying off the driver, and in the total darkness bumbled into the rear of a car parked beside the two beat-up Land Rovers belonging to her father and brothers.

Muttering, Maddie bent to rub her bruised shins. She registered the slam of a car door, and looked up to find the dark, strangely intimidating figure of Dimitri blocking her path.

'Get in the car.'

The terse command sent a shiver prickling down her now rigid spine.

Her mind was a chaotic jumble of shock. What did he think he was doing here? Didn't he understand a simply written statement that their marriage was over? Her throat worked convulsively, and her, 'I'm not going anywhere with you!' emerged on strangled, breathless tones that made her cringe at her seeming indecisiveness. She spoke more firmly, with effort. 'I am going home. Let me pass.' This because he had pinioned her arms in strong, masterful hands, and his touch still had the power to melt her.

'Your family have retired for the night,' he relayed. 'We have discussed the issue and have agreed that it is best that you go with me to my hotel. We need to talk.'

'No!' Maddie bit out in mutiny. 'There's nothing to talk about.'

As she knew from painful experience, he could talk her into believing black was white, and despite her staunch intention to put him out of her life she knew that as yet she was too raw and hurt to keep to that resolve if he decided to use his devilish charm to make her change her mind. For his own despicable ends.

'You can't make me go anywhere with you,' she flung in challenge.

'No?' Still sounding measured—conversational, almost—he parried, 'I have been waiting in that car for over half an hour now, and patience is not my strong point. I have never forced any woman to do anything against her will. But—and this I promise—should you refuse, your family will be homeless by the end of the month. You have the power to stop that happening. It is your choice.'

CHAPTER TWO

WITH deep reluctance Maddie approached the passenger door Dimitri was holding open. Even in the darkness there was no mistaking the grim, forbidding cast of his bold features.

She swallowed convulsively. It was the first time she'd been on the receiving end of his displeasure. The first time he'd shown his true colours. The rest—the smiles, the softness, the warmth and indulgence of the past three months—had been nothing but one huge act, she reminded herself firmly.

Feet dragging to a halt as she reached the open car door, she sucked in a deep breath. She wasn't looking at him now. She could feel his icy rage. It penetrated her layers of clothing, prickled her skin.

'I'm waiting.' Then his voice softened. 'I will take you to your parents first thing in the morning, I give my word. Until then it is best they relax in the belief that we are sorting our own problems out.'

'Why? They're not children in need of fairy tales!'

'I will explain.' His voice hardened with impatience. 'But not here.'

The line of Maddie's mouth grew stubborn. Used

to having his every whim catered to immediately, Dimitri Kouvaris didn't *do* waiting. Well tough. It was time he learned.

Ignoring him with some difficulty, she managed to get her mind back on track. She had two options. She could stick to her guns—walk on up to the cottage, rouse her parents, and ask them what the hell her soon to be ex-husband was talking about. How could he threaten to make them homeless? He was talking rubbish, surely?

Only he didn't make idle threats, she acknowledged with an inner shudder. He had a reputation in business for ruthlessness. What he said, he meant, and pity any person who got in his way or tried to pull the wool over his eyes. She had never seen that side of him before, but it had been there, hadn't it? Cleverly hidden, but there, in a marriage that had had one purpose only. To get an heir. That cold ruthlessness was out in the open now, she recognised, and resignedly plumped for the second option.

Her chin defiantly angled, Maddie slid into the passenger seat, her heart jolting as the door at her side closed with force. If there was the slightest chance that he could carry through with that threat then she owed it to her parents to fall in with his wishes.

For now. Only for now, she promised herself.

The drive to the nearby small market town was accomplished in tight silence. Unlike her journey with the taxi driver, Maddie had no need to give Dimitri directions through the tangle of narrow lanes. The Greek drove and navigated as he did everything else—exceptionally well—and he would have exact recall of the tortuous route between her home and the hotel he'd been using just over three months ago, when he'd embarked on his sneaky campaign to persuade her to marry him.

Unwilling to give headroom to the thought of how absurdly gullible and bird-brained she'd been back then, Maddie clamped her teeth together until her jaw ached, and made herself think of the present.

It was blistering her mind. His totally unexpected presence. His weird threats. If she, loving him with a depth that had shaken her, could take the sensible course, end their marriage and walk away then why couldn't he? It would be so much easier for him, given that he had never loved her in the first place, had seen her only as a walking, fertile womb.

Her smooth brow furrowed as she tried to find an answer. She had genuinely believed that, knowing her decision to end their marriage, he would have shrugged those impressive shoulders and consigned her to history. A swift divorce—made simpler because of her firm intention not to ask for any financial settlement—followed smartly by a marriage to another such as she—a gullible little nobody from an ordinary, fairly simple but prolific family. The sort who wouldn't know how to stand her ground against the mighty Kouvaris empire when she found herself in the divorce courts, her child given into his custody.

Her face flamed with a mixture of outraged pride and humiliation. She should have cottoned on—at least suspected his motives all those months ago. It had been there right under her nose if only her starstruck eyes had been able to see. His questions, which had given him the information that she came from undeniably fecund stock. Their—what had his snooty aunt called it?—their hole-and-corner wedding. And the lack of anything as romantic as a honeymoon. Not that she'd minded that. She had assured him that she understood perfectly when he'd pleaded that pressure of work meant he had to be in Athens, soppily saying that where he was was where she wanted to be. She'd been too blinded by love to read anything into any of it.

Her hands clenched, her fingernails cutting into her palms. Looking back, she just didn't believe herself! How could she have thought, for one insane moment, that a man as knock-'em-dead gorgeous, charismatic, sophisticated, rotten rich and frighteningly clever would want to tie himself for life to an ordinary-looking, low-status nobody like her?

As he brought the car to a halt in front of the small town's only hotel Maddie made herself a set-in-concrete promise. If her devious husband tried to make her change her mind, because he'd decided he didn't want the delay of even a quickie divorce and then the tiresome chore of hunting down another sucker, with the tedious expenditure of all that seemingly effortless charm to get her to marry him, and had decided he'd be better off sticking to the brood mare he'd got—which, thinking about it, was the only motive possible for him being here at all—then she would resist all his attempts to her very last breath!

With scarcely controlled impatience Dimitri fisted the ignition key and exited the car, reaching the passenger side in a handful of power-driven strides.

He wrenched the car door open and ordered, 'Come.' He had to use every last ounce of self-control to stop himself from hauling her to her feet. In the space of twenty-four hours his wife had changed from a voluptuous, adoring wanton to an ice-cold stranger. And he didn't know why—although he had strong and utterly distasteful suspicions. It was driving him insane. And no one, not even his wife, would be allowed to do that!

As if she sensed the stirrings of his volcanic anger, Maddie moved. Slowly swinging her feet to the ground, she exited the car and stood, facing the timber-framed façade of the hotel. The light from above the main entrance illuminated her. She was wearing jeans and a lightweight jacket, a leather bag clutched in one small hand, a mutinous twist to her mouth.

Dimitri cupped an unforgiving hand beneath her elbow and headed to the main door. If he bent his head he could tease the mutiny away, feel those lush lips tremble beneath his own, flower for him. The gateway to paradise. She liked sex, more than met his demands. But no way would he oblige—now, or in the foreseeable future. That would be part of her punishment!

No, the sex hadn't been feigned. Everything else in their marriage had been, though. Starting with her wedding vows, uttered with her eye on the main chance. He was ninety per cent sure of it. Three months of her life in exchange for a settlement that would keep her in luxury for the rest of her days. Logically, it was the only scenario that remotely fitted in with what she had done—and, heaven knew, he'd racked his brain to try and find another, coming up with a big fat zero.

She would not do that to him!

He removed his hand from her arm as if even that connection was poisonous.

Maddie shivered as the heavy main door swung closed behind them and he strode away from her. She hadn't wanted this confrontation; it had been forced on her. No wonder her nerves were going haywire, adrenalin pumping through her veins. He was rigid with anger, she recognised. And she could understand it.

He was a busy man, a driven man. Amanda had told her, in one of her long, chatty phone calls after Maddie had returned to England that first time, that Dimitri Kouvaris had pumped her for information. About her, about her family. Stupidly, the knowledge had excited her, made her feel almost special. How he would hate the waste of his time. Not that it had taken much of that, she recalled with a sickening lurch of her tummy. Five days later, after having gathered the necessary information from her unsuspecting friend, he had charmed her into a state of besotted adoration with very little effort.

No, he would view the three months of their marriage as an unforgivable waste of his time and effort. And it *would* have taken an effort on his part to treat a peasant as if she were a princess, she decided with a resurgent cynicism. As for the other—the sex—trying to get her pregnant at every opportunity with no result, while thinking of the time when he could get rid of the wife he didn't love and marry the woman he *did* love, must have infuriated him.

He'd hidden it well. She had to give him that.

But now it was showing.

Thing was, was she brave enough to handle it? Discover what he meant by those threats? And the answer was, she *had* to be.

At this late hour the hotel foyer was deserted, the

lights low, adding another layer of atmosphere to the heavy exposed beams and oak panelling of what had once been a coaching inn. The night porter had emerged from his cubby-hole behind Reception and was handing Dimitri a key. A few inaudible words were exchanged, and then he swung round on his heels and faced her, his stance disdainful, coated in ice.

Sucking in her breath, she obeyed his curtly expressive hand gesture and made herself move towards him, her head high. True, she wasn't here of her own free will—but she'd be damned if she was going to let herself down and act like a victim.

'We can talk in the lounge.' Her voice as firm as she could make it, Maddie gestured towards a partly open door. The steel grille was lowered over the bar, but there were comfy lounge chairs grouped around the tables, and the light from the foyer gave sufficient illumination.

Totally ignoring that sensible suggestion, just as if she'd never spoken, Dimitri started up the uncarpeted broad oak staircase, and Maddie, biting back a howl of fury, followed.

Arrogant low-life!

Still seething, Maddie caught up with him as he opened a door and reached in to switch on a light.

'In.'

Her stomach clenched painfully. This icily intimidating side of him was alien to her. But she was going to have to get used to it—at least for as long as it took him to spell out what had to be, surely, his groundless threats.

Slightly comforted by that slice of common sense, Maddie stepped into a room that looked as if it hadn't had a makeover since the sixteenth century. And all the better for it, she approved, making an inventory of the jewel-coloured rugs laid over wide, highly polished oak boards, the ornately carved four poster bed and linen press, the tapestry-like curtains. It took her weary mind off being here with the husband she had loved to distraction and now hated with a vehemence that made her bones tremble.

An overnight bag stood at the foot of the bed. So he must have checked in here before driving out to her parents' home. To wait. Somehow he had known that she must contact her folks on her arrival back in the UK, stay with them or in the vicinity until the divorce came through, she deduced tiredly—though the reason for his precipitate actions escaped her. And how had he arrived ahead of her?

She would have already been waiting for her delayed flight when he'd returned at lunchtime, making for the bedroom as usual and more of the sex he was so good at—the hoped for end result his son and heir—and finding her note instead.

And yet he had been ahead of her, waiting for her. His private jet—of course! Why hadn't she remembered that? Because she'd never rated the outward signs of his financial clout, only the man himself. The super-wealthy had the means for getting things done that humble peasants could only dream of, she decided with resignation, as a firm hand in the small of her back propelled her towards two wing chairs at opposite ends of a low, dark oak table.

She sat, was grateful to. She couldn't remember ever feeling this weary and drained in her life before. Dimitri was hovering over her, his hands in the trouser pockets of his superbly tailored pale grey suit, the fabric pulled taut against his pelvis.

Smothering a groan as a hatefully familiar, ultra-responsive frisson lurched through her entire body at his sexy magnetism, Maddie closed her eyes to shut him out. She didn't need that kind of betrayal from her own body—not now, not ever again. All she needed right now was the healing oblivion of sleep.

And if he was waiting for her to ask him to explain himself, to instigate some kind of conversation, then he could wait. This—whatever it was—was his idea, most certainly not hers.

She heard the discreet knock at the door, sensed him move and opened her eyes reluctantly in time to see the night porter place a tray on the table. Something changed hands—a tip, presumably—and Dimitri sat in the chair opposite, surveying her with golden eyes lacking in expression over a lavish platter of sandwiches, a wine bottle and glasses.

Her lungs aching with the effort to hold back a hysterical peal of laughter, Maddie gripped the arms of her chair to keep herself grounded. An outraged husband about to read the Riot Act and explain vile threats to his runaway wife and the first thing he thinks about is his stomach! The situation was farcical!

But there was nothing off-the-wall about his containment as he poured wine into two glasses and slid two sandwiches onto a delicate china plate and put it in front of her. There was even a hint of a smile on that devastatingly handsome mouth as he imparted, 'If, like me, you haven't eaten since breakfast, you'll need this.'

'Not hungry.' Maddie eyed the food with disdain,

her stomach rolling sickly as she experienced total recall of precisely *why* she hadn't been able to face breakfast, or the thought of food since then.

As usual, he had risen first, full of vitality, leaving her to come awake more slowly, stretching luxuriously in the rumpled bed, sated with the passion of the night before. She had pushed away the uncomfortable thought that their time in bed together was the only time she was truly happy. The rest of the time everything conspired to make her feel purposeless, a thing of little use, an unsavoury intruder into a rarefied atmosphere.

She had followed him down, a silk robe covering the naked voluptuous body he always seemed so wild for—gratifyingly belying the snide rumours and wicked lies she'd been fed just lately—expecting to share a pot of coffee with him before he left for his high-tech head office in the city, as she always did. She'd needed her Dimitri fix to carry her through the morning before they enjoyed a long and intimate lunch-break together.

Slipping silently into the sunny room where the first meal of the day was taken, her eyes had gone soppy at the sight of that tall, commanding figure, dressed that morning in pale grey trousers that hugged his narrow hips and skimmed the elegant length of his strongly muscled legs, his white shirt spanning wide shoulders, his suit jacket draped over the back of one of the dining chairs.

His broad back to her, he had been speaking into his cellphone. He hadn't seen her—as the contents of a conversation that was to turn her life upside down soon evidenced.

'Be calm, Irini,' he had soothed. 'We discussed this. It will take time. Please be patient.' A short silence from him, then, decisively, 'I will be with you in less than five minutes, and of course I love you. You are—' Another silence while he had listened to what was being said, then, his voice full of soft emotion, 'Be calm, sweetheart. Five minutes.'

Heart pounding, blue eyes stunned, she'd watched him snatch up his suit jacket and stride out through the open French windows, heading for the woman he *did* love, leaving the woman who was just a commodity clutching the doorframe for support, the lies turned into truth, the rumours into hard, hateful, hurtful fact. The last straw.

At least he hadn't lied. He had never said he loved her, had he?

Now, Dimitri helped himself from the platter, golden eyes assessing beneath the thick dark sweep of his lashes. She was pale, her skin ashen beneath the light golden tan, the band of freckles across her nose standing out starkly. He had always found those freckles endearing—those and the caramel curls now delightfully tamed by the best hairdresser in Athens. The fierce, rapacious need for her wildly sensuous body, his need to soften the raging heat of lust into something infinitely more tender, more fulfilling, made him furious with his body for responding to his thoughts. Blisteringly angry with her for what she had seemingly proved herself to be, he said, with more force than necessary, 'Eat before you pass out.'

Never one to respond positively to anything smacking of bossiness or bullying, Maddie flattened her mouth stubbornly. She crossed her arms over the breasts he had once said he worshipped, and clipped out at him, 'I didn't come here to eat with you. I came because you made threats against my parents and I demand to know how you think *you* can threaten them.'

'So, she finally speaks.' Dimitri was lounging back now, holding a wine glass in one beautifully crafted hand. His voice was smooth as silk he told her, 'No one makes demands of me—not even my wife. Understand that and you'll be a wiser woman.'

With an effort he kept his cool. She had never asked for anything—had made *no* demands. Hadn't needed to. He'd given her everything, and gladly. High status, an assured position in Greek society, wealth beyond avarice, jewels—and she'd thrown the lot back in his face.

His heart thumped with the outraged anger of savaged pride. Because she wanted even more. The sort of divorce settlement that would keep her in luxury for the rest of her life without the burden of having a husband. Until she came up with another plausible reason for leaving him, it was the only motive that made any sense.

He was taunting her, Maddie deduced with mounting horror, her skin crawling with the onset of panic. No doubt he would tell her what he'd meant by that threat in his own good time.

But she didn't *have* time, she thought wildly. Draining tiredness, the beginnings of a thumping headache and the awful emotional trauma of the day meant that any minute now she would break down, scream and throw things, or dissolve in floods of helpless tears, betraying how desperately unhappy his betrayal and cynical manipulation of her had made her. She wouldn't be able to prevent it happening if she had to suffer this unwanted confrontation, this not knowing, for much longer.

Dimitri set his glass down with an irate click. The gold of his eyes frosted. Time she learned she couldn't make him look a fool, shame and dishonour him. Time she knew who called the shots.

'You are my wife. There will be no divorce. You will return with me to Greece. If the marriage ends at some time in the future, as seems likely, then *I* will be the one to end it. I demand that much. I will not be made to look a fool in front of my friends and colleagues.'

Because she hadn't given him an heir, Maddie translated, chilled to the bone by his harshly decisive delivery. Hanging on to her rapidly fleeing composure, she managed, 'You can't stop me suing for divorce. Or make me go anywhere I don't want to be.'

Fully expecting a blistering statement of the opposite—because the rich and the powerful had ways of getting everything they wanted—she was speechless when he gave a slight shrug of his magnificent shoulders and uttered blandly, 'True.'

With one hand he loosened his tie and settled back in his seat, graceful in his relaxation. He was more gorgeous than any man had a right to be, she decided in utter misery—then gave herself a sharp mental kick. The days of her overwhelming love for him were over. He was no longer the light of her life, and she no longer felt herself melting inside when she looked at him.

'But?' she all but snapped at him. It wasn't in the nature of the beast to simply cave in. There had to be a 'but'.

There was.

'*But*, if you follow that road be sure that your parents will be homeless by the end of the month. It's in my power to prevent that happening. I will do so—but only if you agree to everything I ask of you. And if you think that you can divorce me, claim a large settlement and help your parents financially, live the high-life, forget it. Any lawyer I employ will make sure you receive absolutely *nothing*.'

CHAPTER THREE

APPALLED by that implied insult, Maddie could only stare at him, feeling her face redden. It showed how little he thought of her! Was proof—if she had needed any after what she'd been told—that outside the bedroom he viewed her with contempt, a necessary evil.

She fisted her hands in her lap—a labourer's hands: short nails, slightly callused palms, as his aunt had commented with acid—and took a long breath. She wasn't interested in his insults. He couldn't hurt her more than he already had done, and she certainly wouldn't lower herself by telling him she'd had no intention of asking him for anything except her freedom because he wouldn't believe her. Why waste her breath when there were more important questions to ask?

The eyes she at last dragged from the cynical gold of his fell on her untouched wine glass. With the distinct feeling that there was worse to come, she reached forward, swept it up and swallowed a long draught. The rush of alcohol into her bloodstream helped her to challenge him, 'I don't believe you. Prove it. Why should my parents lose their home? Why don't we go back right now and ask them?'

'At this hour?' Dimitri drawled, as if hearing words from a total idiot, and leaned forward to remove the half-empty wine glass from fingers that threatened to shatter the delicate stem. He set the glass down on the table and edged the plate of untouched sandwiches further in her direction. 'They are sleeping, happy in the knowledge that we will have kissed and made up after our lovers' tiff and, almost as importantly, that I will help them out of their present difficulties. They have a load off their mind—isn't that how you English would put it?'

Torn between outrage that he should have made light of her precipitate flight back to England and the need to know what the so-called difficulties were, she chose the latter as being far more pertinent.

'What difficulties?' she got out, regretting the urgent note in her voice, but wanting to get it out into the open and get out of here. Away from the man she could no longer stand being near to. 'Tell me!' she pressed, with fuming vehemence, because he seemed to be intent on keeping his mouth shut and his ace up his sleeve, and was looking at her as if she were an object of mild scientific interest.

Dimitri blinked once, then twice. What was that old-hat come-on? *You look magnificent when you're angry!* In this case it was spot-on! However…

Seething with sheer frustration, Maddie watched him tilt his arrogant head, veil his brilliant golden eyes and steeple his fingers as he recited, in a tone so matter-of-fact it made her blood steam in her veins, 'Your father has reached retirement age. The company he works for has terminated his employment, and with it his tenure of the cottage. The accommodation is required by the groundsman who is to take his place, apparently.'

'They told you this?' Maddie asked thinly.

She felt sick. It could be so true. Six years ago old Sir Joseph had sold the Hall and its estate to a business consortium who had turned it into an upmarket conference centre, complete with a golf course, indoor swimming pool and sauna, clay pigeon range and access to excellent trout fishing. Her dad hadn't liked the new regime. Had missed Sir Joseph and the relaxed chats they'd enjoyed over a whisky and a pipe apiece as they discussed estate matters in the cluttered estate office. On one of the last of those occasions the elderly man had confessed that it was time he moved on. He didn't want to, that went without saying. But he couldn't keep up with overheads, he wasn't getting any younger, and he had no family to take over. Miserable situation, but there it was.

But a job was a job, as Dad had said, and the cottage was their family home—and hadn't Sir Joseph promised that it would be theirs for as long as they wanted it?

However, that wouldn't sway the hard-nosed businessmen who ran the estate now. Concessions for loyalty, long service, personal liking and respect wouldn't come into it. None of them would have heard the words 'old retainer', and if they had they would have dismissed them as being laughably archaic. Suddenly the threat of seeing her parents homeless didn't seem empty at all.

'Initially your mother told me,' Dimitri verified. 'When I arrived at your home she was obviously upset. I assumed it was because you'd been in touch and told her you were ending our marriage.' He levelled an incisive look at her, the planes of his darkly handsome face hard and unforgiving. 'But that was not so. When I dealt her that second blow of bad news she broke down and wept.'

Maddie's heart twisted. Anguish leapt to her throat and choked her. Both her parents thought Dimitri Kouvaris was the cat's whiskers. Charming, considerate, super-wealthy, a miracle of perfection—the type of husband they could only have dreamed of for their lovable but unsophisticated tomboy of a daughter. Of course Joan Ryan would have been devastated by his news. But if she'd been able to get her side of the story in first her mother's dismay at the marriage breakdown wouldn't have been so absolute. She would have been disappointed that the dream husband had shown himself to be a cynical, manipulating, cruel brute, but she would have been on her side all the way.

'So you arrived, unasked and unwanted, and put the boot in!' Maddie derided at volume, hating him for causing her mother even more distress. She half heaved herself out of the chair, her only thought to get back to her parents and tell the dark story of why Dimitri had really married a no-account nobody like her. She would do everything she could to help them move, find somewhere else to live, fight the men in suits. Surely there must be a law against that sort of heartless treatment?

'Sit down.' A warning ran like steel through his voice. 'If any *boot*, as you so oddly put it, was used, then it was your foot wearing it. Remember that.'

Subsiding with ill grace, blue eyes simmering with mutiny, Maddie pointed out, 'OK, so you've told me why my folks will be thrown out of their home. But that doesn't change anything. *You* can't do anything about it—'

'True,' he cut across her, smooth as silk. 'I cannot stop them losing the cottage. When the consortium took over your father was required to sign a contract of employment. I saw the document, and I read the small print—which your father failed to do. According to him, he was so pleased to be kept on he signed without reading it. It is watertight. However, if you cast your mind back and think clearly, instead of exploding every two seconds, you will recall that I said I could prevent them being without a home of their own provided you fall in with my wishes.'

She hadn't forgotten—how could she? But, really stupidly, she'd hoped he had. And now she had to sit here and listen—force herself to forget how once she'd loved him and how he'd used that love to blind her to what was in his handsome, cruel head. Difficult to do when faced with all that lean, taut, utterly devastating masculinity, the blisteringly hot memories of how it had once been between them.

She shifted uncomfortably as a responsive quiver arrowed down her spine and lodged heatedly in the most private part of her body. Her face flamed at the uncomfortable knowledge that she still wanted him physically, even as her head and heart hated him.

Mistaking that fiery colour for the precursor of yet another mutinous outburst, Dimitri put in, smooth as polished marble, 'Your parents and brothers have made tentative plans of their own. Not having the wherewithal to buy a property, nor sufficient income as things stand to rent one, Sam and Ben aim to find cheap lodgings. Your parents plan to move into Adam and Anne's spare room while they wait for the council to offer them accommodation—not the most promising situation, I think you'll agree?'

Maddie stayed mute. It was a wretched situation. Her parents had no savings. Any spare cash they'd had had been used to help their children. No matter how her eldest brother and her sister-in-law welcomed them into their small home, things would get tricky. Adam's young family was growing, and space was at a premium and, used to being Queen Bee in her own home, her mother would begin to feel in the way—past her sell-by date. Her parents, bless them, deserved better than that. But she wouldn't give Dimitri the satisfaction of agreeing with him. On anything. Ever again.

Dimitri frowned, slashing dark brows clenching above shimmering golden eyes. Her body language was sheer stubborn mutiny. He would change that. His wife would once again become compliant. It was she who had drawn up the battle lines, and no Greek male could fail to rise to the challenge, meet it and overcome it. Utterly.

Time to deliver his knock-out blow, he decided, harshly ignoring the sharp stab of regret for what they'd once had. Or what he'd *thought* they had, came the cynical reminder.

'When I arrived, your brothers were out, trying to persuade the farmer they rent their piece of land from to agree to rent out the adjoining field and so allow your brothers to produce more and become more profitable.' His tone showed his aggravation as he demanded, 'Are you listening?'

Maddie shrugged, she didn't care if she infuriated him. He deserved it. She was ahead of him in any case. Sam and Ben had often said they needed more land under cultivation. Their organic produce was always in demand. They could sell it twice over easily. But for that they needed more land, another bigger greenhouse, more hours in the day. With Dad out of work it would make sense to expand and let him in as a partner.

Inwardly seething, Dimitri battened down the imperative to shake her until her pretty white teeth rattled—or, more productively, to kiss her senseless until she was clinging, hanging wide-eyed on his every word.

Better yet, and less hurtful to his pride, would be to render the *coup de grace.* Subdue, once and for all the stubborn streak he had never suspected she had.

So his voice bordered on the purr of a jungle cat with its prey within its grasp as he imparted, 'They returned, their plans in ashes. The said farmer had stated that he was selling up. Even renting the piece of land they are currently working might prove to be a problem with a new owner. They could either buy the lot—farmhouse included—or nothing.' He paused a moment to let that further piece of bad news sink in. Then, 'The idea I put to your parents and brothers was this. That *I* buy the farm and they live there and work the land, expand their business.' He allowed himself a small smile. 'To say that they approved the scheme is an understatement. To counter the general non-stop outpourings of gratitude I explained that as they are now part of my family by marriage it is my duty and pleasure to do all I can to help them. Of course,' he completed, in a tone so honey-sweet it set her teeth on edge, 'the whole thing is contingent on your remaining my wife until I, and only I, decide otherwise. Ensuring that I continue to regard your family as my family, my responsibility.'

Her voice faint, Maddie managed, 'That's blackmail! I don't *want* to be married to you. You know I don't!'

'Take it or leave it. Your choice.'

In emotional turmoil Maddie shot to her feet, her fingertips flying to her temples. She couldn't think straight. Her imagination was working overtime as she pictured her family's relief. Even now her mother would be dreaming of furnishing and decorating the farmhouse, of welcoming her menfolk home from the fields with her famous steak and kidney pie!

Her mouth worked with the onset of hysteria, and the edifice of her earlier determination to cut him out of her life crumbled utterly when he rose with languid grace and came to stand in front of her, his voice cool to the point of uninterest as he asked, 'Your choice?' And then, his voice roughening, as if he was uncomfortable with what he had to tell her, he stated, 'And to help you make that choice I'm afraid I have to tell you that less than a week ago your father was taken into hospital with a suspected heart attack.'

He saw her rock on her feet, saw the little colour she had in her face drain away and could have hit himself. Placing his hands lightly on her shoulders, he apologised gently, 'I'm sorry. I could have come at it in a gentler way. The good news is that it was very minor—a warning, and no damage done. Provided he takes his medication and avoids stressful situations all will be well. Your mother told me she was in the process of writing to you to put you in the picture without alarming you unduly.'

This close, she could feel the enervating potency of his lean, hard masculinity, the power of him. That, plus the news of her father's illness, shattered her into honesty, her voice cracking as she cried, 'What choice? I'm between a rock and a hard place!'

'You put yourself there,' he reminded her flatly. 'It's make-your-mind-up time. Return to Greece with me, as my wife, or deny your family the opportunity to make a new life for themselves.' He thrust his hands into his trouser pockets and drawled, 'Tough, isn't it? Turn your back on your hopes of a massive divorce settlement, or—'

'You can be *so* stupid!' she blistered, stung again by his insulting suggestion that she only wanted rid of him because of what she could get out of him. She could put him straight on that score, but the truth would gain her nothing and lose her the only thing she had left. Her pride. And, what option did she really have, especially now that the sneaky wretch had raised her parents' hopes to stratospheric heights? How could she face them with the news that her soon-to-be-ex-husband had withdrawn his generous offer? And heap a bucketload of stress on her father? She couldn't do that to them. Deliberately closing her mind to what she was letting herself in for, she gritted, 'OK—have it your way! And you can keep your obscene fortune intact! Satisfied?'

Not waiting for his response, and hating him for having the upper hand, she turned on her heels, snatched up her bag, headed for the door and said, as coolly as her frustration would allow, 'Take me home. I've got my own key. I can let myself in without disturbing them.'

'You have the regrettable tendency to behave like someone who has had her brain surgically removed—did you know that?' Dimitri enquired silkily, narrowing the distance she had put between them. 'As we have kissed and made up, as far as your parents are concerned, it would look very odd if we did not spend the night together, don't you think?'

Chagrin made her clamp her teeth together. He was right. Give her family one inkling that her husband was blackmailing her and they would close ranks, refuse to accept the lifeline he was offering. And how would *that* affect Dad's health?

It didn't bear thinking about. Her whole system shuddering with reaction, she suffered the indignity of having him remove her jacket, the nerve-racking way those golden eyes drifted over her upper body, where her T-shirt clung to her generous curves, and would have moved smartly away if her legs had had any strength left, and didn't feel and behave as if they were made of wet cotton wool.

'It's been a long day,' he remarked, as casually as if they were an old married couple, perfectly in tune with each other. 'I suggest we turn in. In the morning we will break the good news of our reconciliation to your family, and I will make that farmer an offer he can't refuse.'

He turned away then, a man completely and aggravatingly in control, removing his tie as he reached for his overnight bag, magnanimously offering, 'Use the bathroom first.'

Scooping up her own bag, Maddie scuttled for the *en suite* bathroom and closed the door firmly behind her, regretting the lack of a lock.

It was small, nothing like the luxury she was used to— a huge marbled and mirrored space, an elegant shower room and a spa bath big enough to swim in, surrounded by potted plants with shiny green leaves and glass shelves holding luxurious toiletries—but it was sanctuary.

Her emotions all over the place, she stood for a while, her breathing shallow and fast as she reflected that she'd been right. He'd decided that he might as well get an heir with the wife he did have rather than waste time finding another! And his macho Greek pride came into it, too. Of course it did. *He* would end the marriage when it suited *him*. Anything else would be unthinkable.

Battening down hysteria, she informed herself that she held the trump card. As long as she didn't get pregnant—and she'd make sure he never laid a hand on her again—his hateful plans would take a nosedive. Ignoring her past susceptibility where he was concerned, she felt comforted by the control she had in her hands, and opted for a soothing wallow in the bath rather than the quick shower the lateness of the hour dictated.

She stayed in the water until it began to cool. She had hoped it would soothe her, but it couldn't. The knot of pain inside her intensified until she felt she would die of it. She had loved him so, and now that love had turned to acid, burning her insides. As she heard Dimitri tapping on the door, calling her name, another thought hit her like a falling brick wall, and she jerked upright in sick horror. He had mentioned caring for her family only as long as they were his family through marriage.

Refuse to give him an heir and he would cut his losses and end their marriage.

Give him an heir and still he would divorce her, take her child from her, no doubt using top lawyers and low-down lies to prove to a court that she was an unfit mother.

What price his so-called duty of care then? Her parents and brothers would be out of his property at the speed of light.

She was in a no-win situation. She caught her lower lip between her teeth to stop herself screaming and the door crashed open, to reveal six foot plus of Greek male magnificence, clad only in boxer shorts, and glowering like thunder.

Two paces brought him looming over her as he got out through clenched jaws, 'Why didn't you answer? I thought you might have passed out, hurt yourself! Instead—' Throwing her a look of utter disdain now, he plucked a towel from the heated rail and tossed it to her. 'Cover yourself,' he said, reminding her, to her shame and confusion, that she was stark naked, rivulets of water coursing down her too generous figure. 'If I want what still appears to be on offer, I will take it. But don't hold your breath.'

Humiliated beyond bearing, fingers fumbling, Maddie wrapped herself clumsily in the towel, clambering out of the bath patronisingly aided by one large strong hand around her upper arm.

She shook his supportive hand away as soon as her feet hit the bath mat. He thought she'd planned this. Remembering how in the past she had always responded to her adored and beautiful husband's sexual overtures with greedy, hedonistic delight he *would* think that!

Would think she had decided she might as well enjoy that side of marriage if it would help her towards a large chunk of alimony.

A gold-digger and a harlot!

Smothering a yelp of distress, she darted into the bedroom and stared at the room that had become her prison with wild blue eyes. Impossible to swallow her pride and tell him why she had really left him. Show him the open wounds of the love he had savagely killed, reveal herself to be a victim, still bleeding from his cruel betrayal. Everything in her rebelled against it.

Let him think she wanted a large part of his fortune if he wanted to. But let him think she still wanted him sexually? No way!

In next to no time she had whipped the patchwork quilt off the bed, leaving him with the duvet, snatched one of the pillows and curled herself into a ball on the floor, a bundle of misery as she contemplated a future that looked bleak from every angle. She was fighting tears as she heard him give a low, derisive laugh when he exited the bathroom and encountered her sleeping arrangements, heard the dip of the mattress as he availed himself of the comfortable bed.

And, on a surge of rage, she wanted to go and hit him! Silence.

A thick silence that expanded suffocatingly as the floor beneath grew harder and sleep was impossible to find.

Unable to handle the fact that he should be sleeping the sleep of a man who had got his own way, while his subjugated commodity of a wife lay on the floor like a pet dog, she shot at him, 'Tell me why you would go to so much trouble and expense to keep a wife who only wants rid of you! It doesn't make sense!'

To her it did. Perfect sense from his point of view. But she wanted to force the truth out of him. All she got was a drowsy but blood chilling, 'You are my wife. You will stay my wife until I decide otherwise. There is nothing more to be said on the subject.'

CHAPTER FOUR

As THE chauffeur-driven limo eased to a well-bred halt in front of the magnificent Kouvaris mansion Maddie woke with a start, then momentarily stilled in shock when she discovered that her comfortable pillow was Dimitri's wide, accommodating shoulder, his close proximity teasing her senses with the sensual heat of him, the evocative scent of his maleness.

Extricating herself from the curve of his supporting arm with more haste than dignity, Maddie hurled herself upright. The last thing she remembered was their being met off the Kouvaris jet at the private airstrip by Milo and the limo, then collapsing onto the soft leather upholstery, overcome by black waves of fatigue.

He was still too close. She could sense him watching her in the gathering evening dusk. Gloating now his prey was firmly back in the steel web of his making? His pride demanded that he would end the marriage at his convenience, not at hers. He'd made that very plain.

Fumbling for the door release, she all but fell out onto the wide gravel sweep, her stomach full of butterflies on speed.

'You are now in haste to reclaim your position as

mistress of our home, when yesterday you couldn't wait to leave it, and me?' Dimitri queried in dry amusement, taking only seconds to reach her side and cup a proprietorial hand beneath her elbow.

'That's not funny!' she objected unsteadily, knowing she was too exhausted and feeble to shake his hand off with any hope of success, but standing her corner. 'I just want to go to bed and sleep—alone,' she qualified with pointed emphasis. 'It's been a long day.'

A long, hard, horrible day, she thought with misery. Roused from a scant hour of sleep which had felt more like a heavy coma, she had been unsurprised to find Dimitri already up and dressed, speaking in his own language on his mobile, pacing the room with long, unhurried strides, one dark brow had elevated in her direction as she'd unrolled herself with difficulty from the patchwork bedspread, which seemed to have developed as many tentacles as an octopus during the long uncomfortable night.

Reaching the *en suite* bathroom, she'd clung to the washbasin, feeling queasy and light-headed, meeting the hollow look in her reflected eyes with unaccustomed and demeaning resignation. She hated to admit it, but he had won hands down. Was it any wonder she felt nauseous?

She would get her divorce, but only when it suited him. When she'd given him the heir he so desperately needed. Which wasn't going to happen, because no way would she share a bed with him again. So it would depend on how long that message would take to get through his thick, arrogant skull.

When it finally hit him she would be history. And what price her parents' security then?

Remembering her family's combined and over-whelming gratitude when Dimitri had announced that the sale was going ahead, that everything was in the hands of his English lawyer, who would shortly be in touch with theirs, Maddie felt sick.

Somehow she was going to have to warn them that their days on the farm that was now the property of her husband were numbered. She hadn't had the heart to get her parents on one side and give them that slice of bad news, to advise them to start looking for somewhere affordable to rent and promise she would do all she could to help on the financial front because the generous allowance Dimitri had given her was largely untouched.

It would have to wait until her father was much stronger.

While she'd been helping her mother to make lunch, Joan Ryan had asked, 'Is everything all right? Between you and Dimitri? I was horrified when he told me you'd left him. It was just one blow too many.'

Meeting her anxious eyes, Maddie had mentally crossed her fingers. 'Sorry, Mum. It was just a silly mis-understanding. You know how stubborn I can be! I'm going back with him this afternoon. Don't worry about me. Just concentrate on getting Dad to chill out and take things easily.'

And Dimitri's Oscar-worthy act as one half of a newly reunited happy couple after a silly spat had obviously completely allayed her family's anxieties on that score, but it had made her feel sick with loathing him to see the ease with which he wore his cloak of deceit.

'You will behave as I expect my wife to behave. With dignity.' Dimitri's hand now tightened in warning against her arm. 'As usual, we will dine as a family. You have just over half an hour to shower and change. And then, and only then, will you make your polite excuses and retire.'

He couldn't physically force her to sit at that lavishly laid table beneath the glittering chandelier in the vast dining room. Force her to endure the seemingly endless ritual of many courses, the sideways inquisitive looks of the staff who served them, the disdain and disapproval permanently etched on Aunt Alexandra's haughty features. Of course he couldn't, Maddie consoled herself, and tried to believe it as he ushered her through the brightly lit but echoingly empty hall.

Empty until Irini Zinovieff emerged from the arched doorway that led to Aunt Alexandra's rooms. As impossibly svelte and lovely as ever, her tall, slender body was clad in black that glittered, and her scarlet lips parted in a tremulous smile as her eyes locked with Dimitri's and held fast.

What the hell was *she* doing here? Maddie fumed, taking no comfort whatsoever from Dimitri's evident surprise, the sudden drag of air deep into his lungs, the way his body tensed. He hadn't expected her to be here but no way was he going to keep up his former pretence and treat the woman he really loved as a casual visitor. His hand dropped from Maddie's arm as the Greek woman glided towards him, her long white hands outstretched as if in supplication.

Dimitri took her hands and spoke in his own language, the words rapid, questioning. Irini shook her head, mumbled, managing to look contrite and pitiable. Maddie wanted to slap her! And, as if that thought had penetrated their absorption in each other, the other woman appeared to notice her for the first time.

Hard malicious black eyes belied the sweet tone. 'So you decided to come back? Alexandra told me you'd left and wanted a divorce. I came straightaway—' She swallowed, paused and purred on, 'I came to see if I could be of any help. Perhaps she was mistaken?'

Ignoring Dimitri's sudden look of fury, Maddie countered, 'Then I'm afraid you had a wasted journey.'

Her cheeks streaked with angry colour, she headed for the stairs and took them, her head held high. At least it was coming out in the open now. Her all too brief bid to end their marriage had obviously removed the need for him to show her any consideration at all.

Irini only had to call and he'd drop everything to speed to her side, assure her that he loved her.

Irini only had to hold out her hands to him and she was the focus of all his attention. More ammunition— as if she didn't have enough already—to hurl at him when—*if*—she decided to tell him why she really wanted to get right out of his life!

But when she told him she would have to be feeling far less raw and betrayed than she did now, the severe hurt somehow miraculously soothed into indifference. No way would she let her pain show, give his massive ego the satisfaction of knowing how much she had once loved him.

Entering the magnificent master bedroom, the room she had shared with the man she had loved more than life, she felt her soft mouth wobble. Everything in here had once been touched with magic. Now it seemed unbearably tawdry. The soft words, seductive caresses, the loving—all slimy lies. Instinct told her to gather her belongings and seek one of the many other rooms.

Her mouth firmed. No. No way! She wouldn't scuttle away and hide like something unspeakably vulgar, not fit to be seen in polite society. She wouldn't be banished from the sacrosanct master bedroom. *He* would!

Crossing to a gilded table, she lifted the house phone and briskly instructed the English-speaking house-keeper to remove the master's belongings to another room. She replaced the receiver immediately, unwilling to listen to objections or questions, then walked into the sumptuous marble and gleaming glass bathroom to strip and head for the shower while her orders were being carried out.

She had never ordered any of the staff to do anything for her before—hadn't liked to put herself forward to that extent. Hadn't Alexandra more than hinted that her status in the household came slightly below that of the humblest daily cleaning woman? That this first instruc-tion would cause ripples among the staff went without saying. And it would infuriate Dimitri, prick his inbred Greek pride. He would hate to think that he was the subject of backstairs gossip and whispered speculation.

Spiteful? Perhaps. But comforting. Paying him back for canoodling with that woman right under her nose!

It was an edgy sort of comfort that lasted until, towel-wrapped, she returned to the bedroom to find the house-keeper standing just inside the door.

'Anna. Finished?'

'Kyria Kouvaris.' The middle-aged woman's brows met in a slight frown. 'Had you stayed speaking, I would have told you that your husband had already phoned ahead to ask for his things to be moved from this room. It is done already. Of course, if there is something else I can do for you, I am here.'

'Nothing. Thank you.' How she managed to get the words of dismissal out through her tight-as-a-vice jaw Maddie didn't know. Once again he had wrong-footed her, spoiled her tiny revenge—she wanted to throw things! Instead, she dried her hair on the edge of the towel until it stood on end in unruly spikes.

Seething with scalding emotions, she considered her options. Curl up in bed and refuse to budge when Dimitri, black-tempered, tried to command her to join them for dinner? Or behave with dignity and go down to take her place at that table with all flags flying—show them that the lowly little nobody wasn't going to hide in a corner out of shame at her lower-than-a-cleaning-lady status.

As she had seen, Irini was wearing black, the subtly glittering fabric draping her impossibly slender figure. The way she was dressed had pointed to the fact that she wasn't planning going anywhere soon. Her guess was that the woman would be eating dinner with them. So—

Marching to the enormous hanging cupboard, she plucked out the vivid scarlet dress that Dimitri had said should carry an X certificate.

It was one of the mountain of designer clothes he had picked out—confiding after she'd modelled it for him in that exclusive boutique, that he had never seen anything so sexy in the whole of his life. The husky edge to his thickening drawl had made her flush to the soles of her feet, sending her scuttling to model the remainder of the garments he had picked out with her head in an impossible spin, and totally vindicating her immediate mental denial of the things Irini had said to her the night before—the night of the intimidating meet-the-bride party she had been faced with on her first night in Athens as Dimitri's brand-new wife.

She had been living in a fool's paradise back then, she acknowledged with savage self-contempt as she slipped into the dress, the cool fabric lovingly moulding breasts that felt slightly fuller than before, strangely tingly.

Nerves. Just nerves, she told herself as she moodily surveyed her reflection, the way the fine silk clung to her body, hugging her small waist, the narrow-fitting long skirt emphasising the lush feminine curve of her hips, the central slit that denied all demureness displaying glimpses of her legs almost to the level of her creamy thighs.

A wave of cowardice almost had her removing the dress with all haste and finding something much less revealing—until the recollection of how overawed and humble she'd been made to feel when first arriving here as Dimitri's bride stiffened her resolve.

She'd been overawed by the splendour of the mansion, convinced that the whole of her parents' home would fit into the immense marbled paved hall with room to spare.

As if sensing her dismay when faced with a platoon of servants, Dimitri had tightened his arm around her waist and bent his dark head to hers as he'd whispered, 'Courage! They don't bite!', then introduced a tall, imposing woman with greying hair, 'Meet Anna, our housekeeper. Her English is fluent. Be sure to ask her to deal with any changes in household routine you require.'

She had known she wouldn't dare! But Maddie had smiled as the rest of the staff had been introduced, the names going in one ear and out of the other, wondering how she would cope with having a horde of servants to feather-bed her life when she was used to getting stuck in and doing things for herself.

But with Dimitri at her side she had been sure she could do anything! She was a married woman; the fact that her husband was a mega-wealthy shipping tycoon needn't intimidate her. Even now her head was still spinning at the speed and cloaked-with-charm determination of his courtship, the way he'd dispelled her doubts, confessed or hidden, the effortless ease with which he'd made her admit she was head over heels in love with him. She had told her mother that, like him, she saw no reason to postpone the wedding he was insisting on before he had to return to Greece, was secretly appalled by the thought that she might lose him if she insisted that they wait.

But she hadn't been able to help feeling overwhelmed when Dimitri had ushered her into a huge salon furnished with what just had to be priceless antiques, murmuring, 'My aunt is waiting to greet you. Remember I told you that she moved here, into the family home, and brought me up after my parents died? She lives here still, but in her own rooms. She can be a touch acerbic, it is her nature, but take no notice. She will soon grow to value you, as I do.'

But doubts on that score had lodged in her brain as a small, rigidly upright elderly woman had turned from a deep window embrasure. She had been exquisitely dressed in black, her expression like perma-frost. 'So you are the Kouvaris bride?'

Maddie had smiled and held out her hand. It had been ignored. Was that a look of contempt, or was it her normal expression? she had thought hysterically as the intimidating elderly woman had raised one carefully plucked eyebrow. 'I missed the wedding, of course. But then I was not invited. I would have liked to have met your family. In our circles family is of the greatest importance.'

To have given them the once-over, Maddie had translated, trying to keep a straight face even as she'd wondered what the impeccable Alexandra Kouvaris would have made of the tiny village church, Mum's best blue coat, Dad's shiny-elbowed suit, her big rawboned brothers, and Anne—obviously pregnant—trying to control her little son, who thought that sitting still and keeping quiet was an overrated pastime.

Instinctively, she had moved closer to Dimitri, but he had given his aunt all his attention, his voice suggesting a rapid loss of patience as he'd pointed out, 'I believe I explained that, having found Maddie, I saw no point in waiting. I had to be back in Athens on business. To have delayed the marriage until I was freed up would have been intolerable to me. Now I suggest you ask Anna to bring refreshments and then—' he'd turned to Maddie, his eyes not smiling, still touched with annoyance '—I will show my wife over her new home.' As his aunt vacated the room, her head at a decidedly regal angle, he'd said stiffly, 'Her greeting was less than warm. I apologise.'

Maddie had reached for his hand. 'You did warn me! And don't be too hard on her. She's probably miffed because she's been deprived of a big splashy do and a splendid new outfit!'

She'd made light of it then, but all her attempts to reach some kind of rapport with the elderly woman since had come to nothing. Oh, she'd always been polite when Dimitri was around, but on all other occasions she'd been at pains to point out that she wasn't fit to clean her husband's boots.

Not wanting to create family discord, Maddie hadn't complained to Dimitri, had done her best to ignore the insults, to discount what Irini said as pure spite, trying to adjust to her new lifestyle. But gradually, like the dripping of water on a stone, her self-confidence had been eroded, and that overheard phone call had been the final confirmation of her painful suspicions.

It was almost laughable, but on that morning she had made her mind up to unburden herself, tell Dimitri what Irini had said and wait for him to dispel those initial doubts about why a man such as he should be so determined to make a very ordinary girl his wife. Doubts that had been systematically fanned by his aunt. But that phone call had forced her to face the truth.

Thrusting unwanted memories aside, Maddie took a deep, calming breath. A final spray of perfume—far more than she usually wore, but who cared?—and she swept out of the room on the highest-heeled strappiest shoes she owned, her face set in a rictus of a smile designed to portray that she was nobody's fool, and not about to be used.

A smile that vanished without a trace as she neared the partly open door of the vast dining room and heard Alexandra's acid tones. 'Do we wait for ever, nephew? I can't imagine why you brought her back here. Why not pay her off and be rid of her? It's what she wanted. Best for all of us.'

Not waiting to listen to Irini's soothing response or Dimitri's harsh interjection, Maddie marched in, swept a bland look at the three of them, and took her place at the exquisitely appointed table, slightly comforted to see a stroke of dull colour outline Dimitri's angular cheekbones.

He was directly opposite her, with Irini on his left— Irini, whose lips curved sweetly as she turned her head to listen or to reply to what he had said, whose black eyes shot contempt when they occasionally turned in Maddie's direction.

As far as Maddie could tell, her wretch of a husband had forgotten she was there. He certainly paid her no attention, addressing his remarks to the others, the flush gone, his startlingly handsome features pale now beneath his habitual tan.

On her right, Alexandra imparted, 'I am spending August in Switzerland this year. No one who is anyone stays in Athens; the heat is unbearable.' There was a rare smile in her voice as she asked Irini, 'And you, my dear, shall you go with your parents to Andros again? Or perhaps I could persuade you to accompany me to the mountains?'

It was the first time Maddie had seen the other woman even slightly discomfited. Colour stained her creamy skin and there was a look of panic in her dark eyes as they turned for reassurance to the smooth brute at her side, the brute—who briefly covered one of the Greek beauty's hands with his own and imparted, 'I believe Irini has plans of her own. Isn't that so?' receiving a subdued nod of assent with a smile of satisfaction.

'Ah—a mystery!' Alexandra smiled archly and Maddie, her mouth tightening with humiliation, guessed that the old lady thought those plans included Dimitri. She was probably right.

It was no secret that the childless, unmarried Alexandra doted on Irini, the only daughter of her oldest friend. She regarded her almost as her own, and had hoped for a marriage between her nephew and the daughter of the highly established Zinovieff family. Greek marries Greek; money marries money—as she'd once scathingly told Maddie.

Just another drip of the poison she'd been careful to keep hidden from her nephew. Barbs Maddie hadn't repeated to Dimitri, not wanting to cause ill-feeling, because Alexandra was the only close family he had and in Maddie's book family was vitally important. Instead, she'd held her tongue and hoped that the older woman would come to accept her. But that hadn't happened.

Silence fell as plates were removed and bowls of plump fresh figs and glowing dark red cherries were brought to the table, followed by the usual *café frappe*. Dimitri at last stopped dredging up innocuous subjects of conversation and raised his eyes to his wife for the first time since she'd entered the room. It sent hot blood flowing to that part of his anatomy he was determined to ignore.

Theos! If she'd worn that dress hoping to drive him wild, she'd succeeded! Throughout the interminable meal it had taken all his self-control to keep his eyes off her. Just looking at her had him aching for her hot, wildly responsive body! A pleasure that he had vowed he would deny himself—and her—for eternity! She would remain as his wife in title only until she came clean about her true reasons for seeking a divorce.

He'd even had the foresight to phone ahead and ask for his things to be moved to another room. He couldn't share her bed and hope to keep his hands off her.

Despising himself now for his lack of control, the way his body was betraying him, his eyes were drawn to the pert roundness of her full breasts, lovingly shaped by the fine scarlet fabric. The smooth, scented skin of her cleavage invited the touch of his hands, his mouth. *Theos!* Not even his blackest suspicions could stop the minx bewitching him!

A sickening pain twisted round his heart. His marriage had been the most important thing in his life. He'd been working flat out to put everything in order, making decisions that would allow him to delegate more with confidence, freeing him to spend far more quality time with his wife and, hopefully, his children, should he be so blessed.

Unconsciously his long mouth twisted. With a few strokes of a pen his wife had turned his life to ashes. So when his aunt asked, with a simper that grated on his nerves, 'And your plans, Dimitri, what are they?' his voice sounded thick to his own ears as he heard himself reply.

'My wife and I will spend the month on the island,' he stated, and told himself that, alone with her there, he would have the best opportunity to get the truth from her. Discover why she regarded their marriage as disposable when it had meant all the world to him.

He pushed back his chair and rose to his feet in one driven movement, his voice imperious as he demanded, 'Come, Irini, I will see you to your room.' And he would discuss with her the plans for the morning, in minute detail, making sure there would be no mistake, that she fully understood this time that she would need to be patient—do exactly what he said, if there were to be any hope of a happy outcome.

Escaping to her own room—denying the old lady the heaven-sent opportunity to drip yet more poison— Maddie scrambled out of the hateful dress. She'd worn it as a statement. To hold her own. But she hadn't, had she? She'd been ignored, like the object they all thought she was. Honour enough to sit at the same table and not have to squat beneath it, begging for crumbs! And what island had he been talking about? She didn't want to go anywhere with him!

Wrenching off her shoes, she hurled them at the wall, then collapsed in a heap of abject misery on the floor, her arms hugging her knees. It was so blatant—at least he was no longer hiding his real feelings. But he didn't know she was aware of his true motives. She would tell him she did—in her own time.

For now there was enough emotional upheaval going on in her head without adding to it, let alone the fact that 'I will see you to your room' had to be an euphemism for *Let's go to bed!*

CHAPTER FIVE

SLEEP proved impossible. Tossing and turning, Maddie did what she'd vowed not to—relived every moment of the evening of that fateful party.

Faced with the bombshell that the great and the good of Greek society had been invited to meet her, as none of his friends or family had attended the simple marriage ceremony back in England, she had dressed with care in a simple cream silk shift—part of the trousseau Dimitri had insisted on providing for her on a two-day spending spree in London.

She'd done her best to circulate, but had felt a bit like a fish out of water amongst all those sophisticated, wealthy socialites. She had endured the endless questions, the minute scrutiny of her appearance, until finally she'd crept away, her head aching from the constant chatter, just wanting a few moments of peace and quiet to gather herself, locate the self-confidence that was gradually slipping away. She'd walked out onto one of the terraces, found a dark corner and perched on the stone balustrading.

But her peace and quiet had been short-lived, because Irini had appeared, looking fabulous in something ultra-sophisticated and gold, her neck and hands dripping with jewels.

Instinctively her own hand had gone up to touch the sapphire pendant Dimitri had given her on their wedding day, saying it reminded him of her eyes—only reminded him, because no jewel could ever compete with the loveliness of her eyes. A pretty compliment that had warmed her heart then and comforted her now. His name and Irini's had been coupled together, she knew that. But he had chosen *her* she reminded herself, on a burst of self-assurance.

Advancing, Irini had said smoothly, 'I believe you English have a saying. You can't make a silk purse out of a sow's ear. Very apt. You'd better make the most of your days of luxurious living. They'll last only as long as it takes you to produce the Kouvaris heir. And with those big hips of yours it shouldn't take you too long!'

She tilted her head on one side, her slight smile chillingly unkind, ignoring Maddie's gasp of outrage. 'You don't believe me? Then let me tell you a story.' Her voice clipped on, dripping with venom. 'Once upon a time a wonderfully handsome Greek tycoon fell deeply in love with a beautiful Greek heiress. They longed to marry, but sadly the heiress had suffered an accident in early life that left her unable to give him a child. And a child was necessary. The handsome tycoon had no sibling to provide an heir. If he died childless then the vast family empire would pass into the careless hands of a distant cousin, a complete wastrel, or one of his fat, lazy sons. Such a sad dilemma!'

'What's this got to do with me?' Maddie hated the way moonlight touched Irini's face, making her look cold and vicious, hated the way her own mind was taking her, how easily this woman could knock her back.

'Work it out for yourself.' Irini moved closer, her voice lower. 'No? Brain not agile enough? Then let me help you. In their desperation to marry, the lovers found a solution. Not ethical—' she shrugged '—but then don't they say all's fair in love and war? He would look for a fertile woman—foreign, of course, not knowing our language or our customs. She would come from a humble background—from the sort of people who wouldn't have the wit or the financial strength to make trouble. Marry her, produce a child and then divorce her. Keep his heir and marry the woman he loved. Simple? And no need to feel pity for the duped first wife. After all, if she couldn't see beyond the end of her own nose, ask herself why a man such as he would want to marry a common, penniless nobody like her, act on it, then end the marriage and return to her peasant family in England, then she deserves all she gets.'

'You're mad!' Maddie got out through lips that felt stiff and cold, shuddering as a goose walked over her grave. Did the ghastly woman really expect her to believe she was talking about herself and Dimitri? Dressing it up as some kind of sick fairy story? She wouldn't let herself believe it.

Seeming to consider the accusation of insanity, Irini tipped her head to one side, then, pulling herself proudly to her slender height, gave her opinion. 'Not mad. Simply unable to give him a child. If he were a bank clerk and I a shop assistant that would not matter. But in the circumstances—I advise you to think about it and consider your position.' She smiled with a sweetness that sent shivers down Maddie's spine and glided away, heading out of the shadows towards the light spilling from the windows of the mansion.

Maddie shot to her feet. She wouldn't believe a word of that rubbish! She would get back to the party. Right now! Grab Dimitri, find Irini, and force the other woman to repeat that story in front of him! And the more people who witnessed her shame and humiliation the better!

She hadn't got further than a handful of snappy paces towards her objective when Amanda appeared, silhouetted against the light from one of the open tall French windows that marched along the length of the terrace.

'So there you are, Mads! I've been looking all over for you.' She pattered forward. 'I haven't had a chance to talk to you. And Cristos is whisking me off on an extended world cruise tomorrow—six months away—so we won't be able to have a good old girlie chat for ages!'

A big hug, then Amanda held her at arm's length. 'What's wrong, pet? Who's rattled your cage?'

Relaxing just slightly from her bristling determination to make Irini repeat what she'd said to Dimitri, Maddie told her. She and Amanda had shared their feelings, hopes and fears since schooldays. When she came to a tight-lipped halt Amanda gave a low whistle of disbelief.

'That woman's a spiteful cow! I never heard such a load of garbage in my life!' she vowed with vehement assurance. 'She's obviously jealous as hell. She's always been potty about Dimitri, and everyone thought they'd marry eventually—until he showed good sense and fell in love with you. You know, I sort of guessed. When you went back to England he couldn't stop asking questions. About you. Your family, where you lived, all that sort of stuff. Cristos thought he was smitten, too!'

Had he asked how many siblings she had? Checking up on the family's fertility record? Guiltily, Maddie thrust that disloyal thought away, but she did confess, 'He's never said it.'

'Said what?' Amanda pleated her brow.

'Told me he loved me.' It had troubled her just a little, but she'd told herself not to be silly. He'd wanted to marry her, hadn't he?

'So?' The other woman shrugged her pretty shoulders. 'Listen, Dimitri lost both his parents in a dreadful sailing accident when he was just three years old. His aunt Alexandra moved in here and brought him up. She's the achetypal cold fish. He was never shown any loving tenderness, according to Cristos, so it stands to reason that he finds it difficult to verbalise his feelings. But he married you, didn't he? Take my advice, pet. Don't go in there and stage a confrontation. He'd hate that kind of scene. And I wouldn't mention any of it, if I were you. You've been married such a short time and you're only just getting to really know each other. He'll assume you didn't trust him—no matter how often you say you didn't believe a word of it! Trust in marriage is vital, especially when you're dealing with a macho Greek male—believe me, I know!' A final hug. 'Tell him, if you still want to, a couple of years down the line, and he can cross her off his Christmas card list! Now, come on, let's go and party—you've been missing for too long.'

'So where exactly are you taking me?'

Lost in unhappy thoughts, it was the first time

Maddie had spoken since boarding the company helicopter twenty minutes ago, sitting stubbornly tight-lipped, refusing even to look at him.

She loathed him for what he had done to her—was doing. Hated him with a passion that shocked her; she who had never hated another living soul in the whole of her life!

A week had passed since her return to Athens, and Dimitri had been away until late last evening. Leaving her to kick her heels and do her best to avoid Aunt Alexandra, who had made it perfectly clear she didn't want her there.

On that first morning the housekeeper had informed her that he and Irini had left at dawn, and that while he was absent Kyria Kouvaris was to think of her parents.

A message Anna plainly hadn't understood but Maddie most definitely had. Do another runner and her parents could kiss goodbye to any hope of moving onto the neighbouring farm at the end of the month.

The warning that their new home, the business they hoped to expand, would be taken from them some time in the not too distant future would have to be given, of course. But not yet. Not until her father was stronger and could deal with the stress. Almost daily phone calls to her mother had confirmed that he was still taking things easily but got easily tired. He was looking forward to moving into the farm—a move her brothers would oversee, down to the last teacup.

She shifted restively in her seat now and Dimitri said, 'We're going to spend a few weeks on my private island.'

The eventual response was tight-lipped, and Maddie didn't comment. She was as unsurprised that a Greek tycoon should own his own island as she'd been to learn that he'd taken off with Irini Zinovieff.

What had they been doing during that week—apart from the obvious? she questioned wretchedly, increasingly wired up inside. Discussing how best to deal with a recalcitrant wife—a wife who should be providing him with an heir but plainly had no intention of doing so?

And had they come up with some plan of action? Bitten the bullet and decided that he must expend his considerable charm and sexual magnetism to get her into bed again and conceive the child that was so necessary to their plans? Was that why he had returned from his idyll with Irini looking so grim and drained?

Well, he could try. And get no place fast, she vowed, bitterly ashamed of the way her heart turned over inside her breast at the very thought of sharing a bed again with her sinfully wilful, drop-dead sexy husband.

A shame that lasted until the pilot put them down on a smooth area of flower-dotted grass a hundred yards from a stone-built villa, when deep apprehension took over, abating just a little as two figures emerged from the side of the building, male and female, stocky, dark, and beaming all over their seamed nut-brown faces.

Coming down to land, she'd seen no sign of a village or a harbour, just a seemingly impenetrable rocky coastline, steep-sided fields, wooded hillsides, and occasional flashes of silver where streams tumbled through ravines down to the silky azure sea.

Fear of being alone with him gripped her, doubly intense because she knew how easily he could, if he wanted to, cleave through her defences as if they were weaker than ill-set jelly, and drive her wild with sexual excitement, with wanting him, needing him, only him.

But the appearance of the approaching couple made

her let out a shaky breath of relief. A least she and Dimitri wouldn't be completely alone here.

Relief, when it concerned Dimitri Kouvaris, had a habit of being short-lived. A lesson rammed home when he imparted coolly, 'Yiannis and Xanthe caretake for me. In return they have their own home and a small farm on the opposite side of the island. I warn you, they don't speak a single word of English. So if you're planning on begging a boat ride with them back to the mainland it's not going to happen.' He proceeded to greet the couple warmly in his own language. His smile was the one she remembered from the days of her happiness, producing a deep ache in her heart for what might have been, had he loved her and not simply used her for his own devious ends.

Yiannis and his stout wife Xanthe obviously thought the sun rose and set with Dimitri Kouvaris, Maddie thought sourly. But she couldn't blame them. Hadn't *she* been completely bowled over by his effortless charm? So who was she to harbour scorn?

Introductions were made, and Maddie submitted to having both her hands clasped with enthusiasm and returning smiles until her face ached, not understanding a word of what was being said to her.

She was sorry to see the friendly couple go, gathering the luggage the pilot had unloaded and carrying it to the villa, where the main door stood open in welcome. She followed them slowly, leaving Dimitri to exchange a few words with the company pilot.

The heat was intense. Her denim jeans and T-shirt were sticking to her body, and her hair felt heavy and damp on her forehead and the nape of her neck. Inside her breast her heart was heavy. She had no firm idea why Dimitri had brought her to this isolated place, just uneasy suspicions, and she knew she wouldn't like it, whatever it was.

'We could both use a shower.' He had caught up with her, shortened his pace to match hers. Pandering to her northern wilting in the face of the fierce Mediterranean heat? Unaffected, he looked as fresh as a daisy, crisp and cool in stone-coloured chinos and a similarly coloured cotton open-necked shirt.

So she was hot, sweaty, bulgy in the hip and bosom department, and couldn't hold a candle to the cool, elegant sophistication of his lover, who had probably never even gently perspired in the whole of her pampered life. But there was no need to rub it in! Too hot and bothered, too incensed by her own interpretation of his remarks she didn't respond, simply questioned sharply, 'So why are we here?'

For a moment there was silence but for the sound of their footfalls on the paved area beyond the flower-jewelled grass. Then, 'It is generally believed that we are enjoying the honeymoon you were denied three months ago.' If he sounded sour, he couldn't help it. He'd been working all hours towards getting a new business regime on track, towards freeing him up to surprise her with a three-month honeymoon—anywhere in the world she fancied, her choice. This—this confrontation over her wish to end their marriage—was the last thing he'd wanted.

The scornful objection she would have lobbed at him died in her throat as she lanced a glare at him. There was a gritty edginess to his unforgettable features, tension in the line of his mouth betraying inner turmoil.

Did he dislike the situation as much as she did? Was his plan to get her pregnant, provide him with the heir he needed, beginning to sicken him, too? To his dynastic way of thinking an heir was all-important. During their short and head-spinning courtship he had often spoken of his desire to have a family—a desire she had matched back then with a retrospectively cringe-making enthusiasm.

Was there yet another side to this need of his? A long entrenched, driving need for a family of his own because from an early age he hadn't had one? Losing both his parents at such an early age and being brought up by his aunt Alexandra wouldn't have been a bed of roses. As far as Maddie could tell, and backed up by what Cristos had said to Amanda, the old lady didn't have an affec-tionate or compassionate bone in her body.

The odd shift in her mood kept her silent while he escorted her through the house. The cool tiled rooms with vaulted high ceilings contrasted with the heat outside, and the wide white marble staircase with its delicate cast-iron banisters soared up to airy corridors and the room the honeymooning couple would share.

The suitcases had been unpacked, and Xanthe was putting the last of the garments in a vast hanging cupboard, full of smiles, bobs and many words as she made her exit. Not giving the room even a cursory glance, Maddie waited until the door had closed behind the care-taker, then said, 'I know we need to talk—about the divorce.' Her face reddened beneath the chilling impas-sivity of his gaze but she struggled on, disadvantaged by his seeming indifference to what she was trying to say. It made her feel like a low-grade employee asking for a rise in wages she had done nothing to earn. 'But we could have done it in Athens without putting on this farce.'

'So we could. If there were any question of an immediate divorce.'

He was closing that door. Again. The word *immediate* induced panic. She would get her divorce when it suited him. When she had given him an heir. And if he pulled out all the stops to make it happen, then manufactured evidence to prove she was an unfit mother, a feckless wife, she would lose her child, her sense of self-worth, and in all probability her parents and two of her brothers would lose their home and their livelihood. Because if he were as unprincipled and callous as to hoodwink her into a short-term, no pain no gain marriage he wouldn't think twice about pulling the rug from under her family's feet once the need for blackmail was over.

Her feeling of sympathy for his loveless upbringing, his lack of close family, vanished like a snowflake falling on hot coals. He had strolled over to open the louvres on one of the tall windows that marched down the length of the room. As insouciant as all-get-out, he turned to face her, his hands in the pockets of his chinos, pulling the fabric tight against his hips.

Giving her a glinting look she couldn't read, he drawled, 'Tell me, why do you want a divorce?'

Her face crawling with colour, because that stance shouted animal magnetism and she wanted to be immune but wasn't, she shot back, 'Because I don't want to be married to you! Haven't I made that plain?'

'I think not. I think you don't entirely know what you *do* want.'

He had moved closer now. Golden eyes smouldered, transfixing her like a rabbit in the headlights of an oncoming car.

'I think—' And the thought had only just occurred to him, making him feel as if he'd received a hefty thump in the gut. Had she been in two minds when she'd left him? Half wanting to get her greedy hands on a handsome slice of alimony, the other half regretting the unlimited sex she'd so obviously enjoyed as his wife?

Even now she was giving off provocative vibes. Those emminently kissable lips were parted, her eyes a sultry gleam of sapphire beneath dense dark lashes, the dampened fabric of her T-shirt was clinging to her spectacular breasts—

Theos!

His hard, lean features rigid, Dimitri blanked off that train of thought. The little witch could turn him on without even trying! Pushing his thoughts into less troubled waters, he let his eyes meet hers with controlled intensity. 'You were a virgin when we married. Having sex with me opened up a whole new unguessed-at world of sensation. Sensation you were always eager to indulge in.'

Maddie clasped her hands behind her back to stop herself from hitting him. 'Are you trying to make some sort of point?' she flung at him, loathing him for making her sound like a budding nymphomaniac, and caught her breath in outrage as he gave her another slice of his twisted mind.

'In the process of trying to see inside your pretty head, I am merely stating facts and my suppositions arising from them, since you refuse to tell me why you ran out on our marriage, leaving me trying to make sense of it. You married me. Why? For the life of luxury you knew I could give you? And then, after you experienced it, for the sex?'

Mortified beyond belief, Maddie couldn't speak—couldn't say a word in her own defence. Not only a gold-digger but a nymphomaniac, too!

And there was more. A grim cast to his mouth, he queried flatly, 'Did you make your wedding vows already scheming to sue for divorce after a few months? To secure yourself a slice of alimony that would enable you to lead a life of luxury? And when the time came to carry it out did you realise that you would miss the only other thing you valued in our marriage? The sex.'

'You are so sick!' Maddie spat out in immediate and instinctive repudiation, struggling to understand why he was doing this. Shouldn't he be doing what she had most feared? Sweet-talking her, coaxing her back into the marital bed and trying to convince her that their marriage was viable, instead of accusing her of the most horrible things?

Her throat convulsed, and to her shame she felt hot tears sting the back of her eyes. Was she so inexcusably weak where he was concerned that she actually—in the secret centre of her heart—*wanted* him to try to coax her, convince her?

Her mind in turmoil, Maddie simply stared at him as she grappled with a thought that was far too uncomfortable to be lived with. Of course it wasn't true. Why on earth would she want him to—to coax her?

'And you still want me,' Dimitri countered. His brilliant golden gaze rested explicitly on her mouth, making her bones turn to water and her breasts stir in instinctive response so that she just knew the engorged peaks would be plainly visible beneath the thin, sweat-dampened fabric of her top—a sensation so well remembered and now so unwanted that she scrambled for what was left of her wits and threw back at him, 'If I still wanted to share your bed, as well as enjoy a life of spoiled-rotten luxury, I wouldn't have left you, would I? You're talking rubbish!'

'Am I?' He moved closer, so close that to her extreme distress Maddie felt her own vastly annoying body strain against her will—strain to close that small distance and melt into the hard, dominating maleness of him. 'Correct me if for once in my life I'm wrong,' he asserted, with an arrogance she could have killed him for, 'but I believe that if you weren't in two minds, had truly wanted to end our marriage, you would have made sure you weren't so easy to find. Headed for some place other than the glaringly obvious.' A sardonic fly-away black brow rose. 'I'm right, aren't I?'

Floored by his truly incorrect deduction, Maddie quivered helplessly. She hadn't looked on her flight from their marriage in that light; she simply hadn't taken his Greek pride into account—the pride that would force him to track her down, demand answers.

All she'd wanted was the comfort of the familiar, the people who really loved her, somewhere sympathetic to lick her raw wounds. She'd been ridiculously easy to track down. He'd even arrived at her destination before her! Made sure she returned with him!

'That being so,' he continued, as if she'd humbly agreed with his assessment of the situation, 'I believe that the larger part of you, deep down, prefers your assured lifestyle as my wife because it has the added bonus of great sex on tap, rather than the insecurity of not knowing how great or small a settlement your lawyer could squeeze out of mine, and the bother of finding some other stud to satisfy your sexual needs.'

'No!' Maddie had difficulty finding her voice. She hadn't a clue which accusation she was denying, and wondered what further character assassination he could come up with next to cover his own vile misdemeanours.

'Yes,' he overrode her smoothly. 'You do still want the pleasure I can give you.' An assured smile tugged unforgivably at the corners of his wide sensual mouth. 'Shall I prove it?'

CHAPTER SIX

SHE stared up at him, wide-eyed, dry-mouthed, heart jumping, and pushed out a chokily ambivalent, 'No—' But she shuddered helplessly as he closed the gap between them and enfolded her in his arms.

Blood racing in her veins, Maddie raised her hands to push him away, make him keep his distance. Because distance between them meant she was safe from her own deplorable weakness where this one man was concerned. But without conscious effort she found her small fists unfurling, her palms flat against his broad chest, and the heady warmth of him sent rivers of sensation skittering through her body, paralysing her.

'I think, *yes*,' he corrected her, his eyes a golden shaft of confident male mastery in his leanly handsome features, his clean breath feathering her skin as he lowered his dark head and claimed her mouth with breathtaking expertise, teasing her lips apart with no effort at all, meeting no resistance, until she was kissing him back with an aching hunger she was completely unable to disguise or pretend didn't exist.

Defences shattered out of existence, she gasped

raggedly at the wildly erotic sensation that engulfed her as his strong hands lowered to pull her hips in contact with his hard, demanding arousal, the memories of what had happened since he'd dropped everything to fly to the side of the woman he loved expunged in the wild fever of blind, unthinking sexual excitement.

This was how it had always been. His passionate lovemaking allaying the doubts and insecurities that had grown during those three months at his home in Athens, fuelled by Irini's far-too-frequent presence and Alexandra's poisoned snobbery.

'This is how it should be for us, yes?' Dimitri breathed, his hard thighs pressed against hers as he eased her backwards towards the massive luxurious bed. His mouth invaded hers again with sensual know-how, his voice thick with satisfaction, as if he knew about the burning fire that pooled in the heart of her, that licked the flesh of her inner thighs with liquid, searing heat as he assured her with pure Greek male confidence, 'You know it is.'

The part of her that murmured feebly about self-preservation, the part that told her to deny it, was woefully weak, and even those semi-formed hazy urgings evaporated beneath the heat of what his clever hands were doing. Lulling her into a false sense of security, as they had always done. She tried to fight it. Her breath caught. It was impossible.

Sliding beneath her T-shirt, curving around the engorged, unbearably sensitised globes of her breasts, his long fingers gently teased the tight crests. He knew what this did to her, he *knew* it, and he was using her treacherous body against her.

He was using unfair tactics, playing dirty—and that was her last semi-coherent thought as he eased her back on to the bed, removing her flattie sandals in one fluid movement before turning his smouldering attention to divesting her of her T-shirt. And, fingers clumsy in her complete capitulation, in her unthinking eagerness to aid her own downfall, she helped him, writhing in intolerably aroused abandonment as he dealt with the fastenings at her waistband and slid the denim fabric, the sheer silk of her panties, slowly and tantalisingly down over the swell of her curvy hips, exposing her ripe nakedness to his incandescent golden gaze.

'So beautiful,' he murmured thickly, lowering his head to trail burning kisses from her throat down to the tangle of curls at the apex of her thighs. Helplessly out of control, Maddie gasped wildly, her fingers clinging to the wide span of his shoulders, writhing mindlessly as one of his hands found the melting core of her, cupping her, teasing unbearably, and her voice was a sob of anguished wanting as she cried his name.

'And so willing.'

Distant his voice now, drenching her with icy, scarcely believing shock as he moved away from her, looking down at her splayed nakedness with golden eyes suddenly overlaid with ice.

'You are only with me now for the sex,' he imparted frigidly. 'Sorry, *pethi mou*. But, much as you tempt me, I have to decline the invitation until I know why you left what I believed was a happy marriage and asked for divorce. Until you tell me, you will go unsatisfied. And even then I think I will be strong enough to resist the temptation.'

* * *

The stony track petered out beneath her feet and Maddie stared at the top of a cliff fringed with sparse, thorny vegetation, her heart beating wildly, her mind twisting and turning incoherently.

He had left the room. He had said something about fixing lunch, and something else. She hadn't been listening—hadn't grasped a thing through those shock waves.

The moment the door had closed behind him she'd lurched off the now hateful bed and dragged on her discarded clothing, flying down the curving staircase and out in to the sun. Running.

Running away from him. Running from her shame, from the deep and shameful humiliation he'd so cruelly dealt her. The self-disgust, wave after wave—so much of it she had no idea how to cope with it.

What sort of creature was she to forget his plans for her? Forget he only wanted to use her? To crave the joy of sex with him so much that she would offer it on a plate the moment he touched her?

A silly creature who had loved him once.

Who still loved him?

Her throat closed convulsively as she shook her head in sharp negation. How could she still love a man who, according to his cynical thought processes, had believed that she was only after a fat slice of his wealth in the first place, then, on reassessment, had decided that she might as well have sex thrown into the mix for good measure—a man who would stoop to blackmail to get her back, to get her to resume her brood mare duties?

Frowning, she wiped the sweat from her forehead with shaky fingers. She hated to admit it, but there was something wrong with that line of reasoning. He could have taken her. Just like that. If using her as a walking womb was his only reason for forcing her to return to him, why had he walked away?

A power thing?

To demonstrate that he could have sex with her whenever he liked? To punish her, humiliate her for having had the gross temerity to leave him and say she wanted a divorce? Dimitri Kouvaris was a man who didn't know what it meant to be rejected, who always expected, as of right, to be master of each and every situation.

What else was she to think?

A smothered sob escaped her. The sun was so hot, burning relentlessly down from the piercing blue vault of the sky, that she couldn't think straight.

Below, the blue-green seawater, crinkling onto the shimmering white sand, looked irresistible. The thought of sinking into blissfully cool waters filled her head.

A paved path from the villa led to low cliffs, where shallow stone steps had been cut into the rock for ease of access. She'd ignored it. Too close. She'd needed somewhere to hide, some place where she could get her head straight, escape the awful humiliation of what had happened. Try to forgive herself where her fatal weakness for him was concerned.

During the three short months of their marriage she had lost herself. Lost the independant young woman she'd been before he had swept her off her feet, meeting his passion with her own because only then had her insecurites seemed ridiculous. Now it was time she found herself again.

Heading away, her breath shortening with exertion, she'd cut through a grove of ancient gnarled olive trees and had come out onto parched grassland, scattering a herd of goats. And here, on another clifftop, possibly at least a mile from the villa—and him—she was safe. Safe until she'd pulled herself together and decided to return. To him.

To tell him in exact detail why she'd left him. To grit her teeth and put her pride—the only thing she had left—aside. And end the farce that their marriage had become.

Countless times during those three months it had been on the tip of her tongue to repeat what Irini had said, to ignore Amanda's advice. But something apart from Amanda's sensible advice had always stopped her. The fear that Irini hadn't been lying?

But she had to tell him now. And do her damnedest to hide the hurt that was still so raw it flayed her. Pride at least demanded that much. If she could manage it.

She had to.

In the meantime the cool waters called her. Feeling fresh and clean again would help clear her mind, wash away the still-burning memories that his hands had imprinted on her skin. Unsteadily, she walked closer to the edge of the clifftop. No convenient steps here. Nothing but the rock face, which seemed to shimmer and shift beneath her eyes. But she could do it—climb down, strip off, and walk into the cool, whispering, welcoming sea.

How he'd resisted the temptation of her he would never know. Even as he assembled the makings of a light lunch his body ached for her—for the only woman, the *first* woman, ever to separate his mind from his body, to take him to paradise and far, far beyond. But that way lay madness.

She had left him; she wanted a divorce. Lust he could control. But not the need to know the truth. Until he knew why he would have no peace. Money? The idea sickened him. He'd been the target of too many greedy little gold-diggers in the past to welcome the thought that he'd been well and truly suckered. But, in the absence of any other sensible explanation from her, it was the only viable answer he could think of.

When he'd given her no option but to comply with his demands she'd come back to him decided she would avail herself of the material advantages she could still claim as his wife, plus the thing she had become hooked on, the thing he gave freely. Fantastic sex. He'd just proved it, hadn't he? And he didn't like the feeling.

Carrying the loaded tray, his mouth curling with distaste, Dimitri told himself he'd get a truthful answer if it killed him. Only to discover that she wasn't waiting on the balcony outside the master bedroom, as he'd instructed her to. Leaving the tray on the delicate white-painted cast-iron table, he took in the bathroom. No sign of her having had that shower.

Sulking somewhere because he'd denied her what her eager body had been begging for? With a hiss of impatience he set off to systematically search the empty villa, the grounds behind, the swimming pool and the area around the vine-shaded arbour.

Nothing.

Standing at the head of the steps down to the nearest beach, he scanned the empty sands.

Nothing.

Anxiety made a furrow on his brow. She couldn't go far. The island was a mere five miles by three at its widest point. But the midday sun was ferocious.

His stride, long and swift, took him to higher ground. Beyond the olive grove, Yiannis's goats were scattered. Unused to strangers, something seemed to have spooked them. Or someone.

Moving faster than he had ever moved in his life before, he followed in the direction he was sure she must have taken. Sunstroke or heat exhaustion was a very real danger for someone who wasn't used to the un-forgiving midday climate at this latitude.

His features tight, he cursed himself. He'd needed proof that, denied her first choice of a ton of alimony and her freedom, she had settled for the very real perks of being his wife.

But had she wanted to end their marriage, get him completely out of her life, because she no longer loved him? Because unknowingly he'd done something to hurt or disgust her? But, if so, she wouldn't have been so eager to have sex with him. Making love didn't come into it. Much as the idea repelled him, for her it was all about lust. Sex.

Well, he'd had his proof and he didn't much like himself for it. He was tough in business matters, he'd had to be, but never unfair and certainly never cruel.

Yet he'd been cruel to Maddie—driven her to put as much distance between them as she could manage within the confines of the small island. He despised himself for the first time in his life. He had his proof and it left a sour taste in his mouth, because in getting it he had shattered his code of honour.

And then he saw her. His thumping heart picked up a beat. Her bright head bent, she was too near the edge of the clifftop. The sound of his approach brought her head round and she took a step back, thankfully away from the edge. As he quickened his steps to a flat-out run one hand fluttered up to her forehead, and she swayed, then crumpled in a heap on the ground.

Within heart-banging moments he was at her side, kneeling, cradling her head and reaching into his back pocket for his mobile. Her face was deathly pale, and the delicate skin around her eyes looked bruised. Two calls. His instructions, bitten out, concise. Repocketing the slim phone he lifted Maddie in his arms and began the slow journey back to the villa—slow because he didn't want to jolt her. He promised himself that once she'd recovered from this—sunstroke?—they would sit down and talk like the sensible adults they were supposed to be. No more threats, demands, mind-games.

As they entered the shaded area in the olive grove she stirred, her eyes drifting open. 'It is all right,' he assured her softly, his heart lightening as he saw her colour begin to return. 'You collapsed, but we will soon be back at the villa and Dr Papantoniou will be with you within the hour.'

'I don't need a doctor. Put me down. I can walk.' A feeble attempt to struggle to her feet had his arms tightening around her—which was absolutely the last thing she wanted, wasn't it? She wanted distance between them. She didn't want him to think he had to be kind to her just because she'd been stupid enough to pass out. It was demeaning!

'I fainted. No big deal,' she grumbled fiercely. 'I don't

want a doctor! I skipped breakfast, that's all!' Because once again the sight of food had turned her stomach.

'Save your energy.' His golden eyes were dark with concern and something else she couldn't read as he glanced down at her. 'Just forget your middle name is Stubborn and do as you're told for once, yes?'

After that Maddie saw no point in pitting herself against his iron will, and submitted, with gritted teeth, to being carried through the cool interior of the villa and gently deposited on the huge bed that had been the scene of her recent stomach-churning humiliation.

But she drew the line when he attempted to undress her.

'I can do that!' She batted his hands away, squirmed round and planted her feet on the floor, snapping tartly, 'If you've decided it's necessary for me to be in bed in a nightie when the doctor calls, to keep up the pretence of not dragging him out here for no purpose, I won't do it—you can go and wait and make your apologies when he arrives!'

Dimitri stood back, but he didn't leave the room. To her utter chagrin he even looked slightly amused, standing watching her, his arms folded over his chest.

Thinking of the invitingly cool-looking sea water, Maddie headed for the shower in the huge marble and glass bathroom. He followed. She was spikily aware of those unreadable eyes pinned on her, and as the only slightly warm water sluiced over her grateful body her anger with him, with herself, increased in proportion to the ache of wanting that flickered and burned deep within.

Damn him! Damn him for making her feel like this. She didn't want it. It was the last thing she needed, she fumed as she grabbed a towel and stumbled back into the bedroom, pointedly sidestepping when he reached out a hand to help her.

Thankfully, the *whump-whump* of approaching rotors brought an end to the situation that was winding her up to explosion point. Glaring at him, pink-cheeked and furious, she watched him move to the door with the innate grace that was so much a part of him.

'Tell him there's nothing wrong with me,' she flung after him. 'And apologise for wasting his time.'

He turned back briefly. 'You are looking better.' There was an almost-smile on his sensual mouth. It made her want to go and smack it away. 'Nevertheless…' He spread his hands, palms uppermost, and closed the door gently behind him.

Intent on making a fool of her. Again. Paying her back in spades for taking off, not doing as she'd been told. The fleeting, unwelcome thought that he might have been genuinely concerned about her was swiftly knocked on the head. He didn't give a darn for her well-being. The only things that mattered to him were any child she might bear for him and Irini. Of course. Mustn't forget the woman he loved enough to do what he'd set out to do—secure an heir, get rid of an unwanted wife and marry where he truly loved.

Totally unwilling to greet the doctor lying like a wilting Victorian heroine on the bed, when there was not a single thing wrong with her, she grabbed fresh underwear from a drawer and a honey-coloured, gauzy cotton strappy sundress from the closet, dressed at speed, and perched herself in a brocade-covered armchair close by one of the windows, picking up a glossy magazine from a nearby table and pretending to be engrossed.

The doctor had other ideas. A serious-looking beanpole of a man, silver-haired and exquisitely dressed, he indicated the bed and carried out an examination that had her squirming with violent embarrassment—because Dimitri was still looming, taut-featured. Though what *he* had to be uptight about Maddie couldn't begin to guess, and wasn't going to try.

As he removed the blood-pressure cuff Dr Papantoniou stood up, smiling. He swung round to face Dimitri. 'Congratulations. My best estimate is that your wife will give you a child in around seven months.' He turned his smile on Maddie. 'You are fit and well, *kyria*. And pregnant. I forbid any further treks in the heat of the afternoon. Remember, you are carrying a precious life inside you. Take gentle exercise in the cool of the day, rest and eat well, and be sure of a happy pregnancy.'

Turning to a shell-shocked Dimitri, he advised, 'I will visit again when you return to the mainland, to arrange tests and make a referral to a top gynaecologist. I foresee no difficulties, but you will naturally demand the very best for your wife and child.'

CHAPTER SEVEN

IF DIMITRI had looked positively shell-shocked at the doctor's announcement, then Maddie couldn't have described what *she* felt. The news that there was a tiny baby growing inside her had made her feel light-headed with something she could only define as fierce protectiveness, all mingled up with the razor-sharp, icy edge of fear.

Because this was the news that Dimitri and Irini had been waiting for. The safe conception of a rightful heir, then—bingo!—get rid of the unwanted wife and marry the so beautiful, so suitably wealthy, so upper-crust love of his life!

How could she have not known? Or at least suspected? But she'd put the extremely scanty nature of her last two periods down to the stress she'd been under, and her early-morning queasiness hadn't occurred often enough to ring alarm bells. If she'd suspected she might be pregnant he could have threatened all he liked but she would *never* have agreed to come back to Greece, she thought wildly.

She would fight him to the last breath in her body before she let him take her baby from her, she vowed staunchly. Then, choking as tears clogged her throat, she buried her head in the pillow. She only realised Dimitri had re-entered the room when his hand touched her shoulder.

Her heart gave a sickening lurch as she twisted round on the massive bed, sitting with her hands tightly wrapped around her updrawn knees to hold herself together, and trying to gather the coherent yet cutting words that would tell him in no uncertain terms she was aware of his sick plans, and that no way would she allow him to bring them to fruition. Even if she did come from a humble background—fit, as his ultra-snobbish aunt would have it, only to scrub his floors— it didn't mean she didn't know how to fight her corner, or that she wouldn't!

But before she could formulate a single phrase, let alone anything approaching a sensible sentence from the mayhem going on inside her head, he took her hands, gently unknotting her savagely clenched fingers, and spoke with a warmth that momentarily drove everything out of her mind and left her gaping.

'Between us we have created a precious new life. There will now be no question of a divorce. And, whatever your reasons for wanting one, I do not wish to hear them. I *will* not hear them,' he stressed with fierce insistence. 'As of the moment your pregnancy was confirmed past differences are forgotten. By both of us,' he stressed again, this time with a blithe arrogance that literally took her breath away.

Just like that! Maddie exploded internally, her gaze narrowing to needle-points of glittering bright blue as she tried to read the golden eyes partially obscured by the thick dark sweep of his ebony lashes. She was as sure as she could be that *divorce* would be the first word to trip smartly off his tongue the moment his son or daughter was born!

Removing her hands from his gentle grasp, she sat on them, speedwell-blue eyes daring him to take them back. He didn't, simply brushed the tumbling silk of caramel curls from her forehead with tender fingers and smiled that slow, devastating smile of his that always before had had the power to send delicious tingles up and down her spine. Now it just made her hate him!

'Today we start our married life afresh, *chrysi mou*. For the sake of our child. And it will be good, I promise. You will want for nothing. Whatever you desire, you will have,' he claimed with extravagant emphasis. 'And now—' he got to his feet '—I will make that belated lunch. You must eat for two now, and I am ravenous! But the food I prepared before will be unfit to eat. I left it on the balcony in my panic to find you.'

The light kiss he dropped on her cheek made her heart leap like a landed fish, and there was anger sparking in her eyes as she watched him walk to the door, turning, giving her that bone-melting smile as he invited, 'Come down and join me.'

The silence that followed his exit was thick with her rage and pain as she vowed she would not be taken for a sucker. Not again!

He had got what he wanted.

Her pregnancy.

Of course he would sweet-talk her—he was very good at it! Brush aside her request for a divorce as the utterings of a retard. Use soft-soap by the bucketful to keep her with him until the child was born. He'd want to keep a close eye on her to make sure she didn't take up sky-diving, get drunk every night, or in any way put his heir at risk!

Swinging her feet off the bed, she stood slowly, straightened her skirt and headed for the bathroom, sluicing her burning cheeks with cold water and dragging a brush through her tangled hair. Staring sightlessly at her reflection, she took several deep, calming breaths.

Dimitri thought he'd got her right where he wanted her. But she would prove otherwise. Always up front— what you saw was what you got—she would change the habits of a lifetime and learn to be as devious as he. She'd had a top-flight tutor in that regard, hadn't she?

Useless to confront him now with what she knew. It was far too late. Pointless to repeat what Irini herself had told her, his aunt's sly hints, or to remind him forcefully of the evidence of her own eyes and ears. The way when Irini was around, he'd always give her the undivided attention she routinely demanded—the way he'd dropped everything on that last morning, not hanging around even to share morning coffee with his wife as he always did. His avowal of love to the other woman would continually haunt her nightmares.

And other things—things that hadn't troubled her one iota before—had fallen into place when she'd been forced to face the truth on that dreadful morning.

Their low-key wedding in the tiny village church, with only her immediate family invited to witness the event, for instance. As if he was ashamed of marrying so far beneath him and regarded the ceremony as a necessary evil, the tedious preliminary to a hopefully short-lived marriage that would provide him with what he really wanted.

Greeks made a great celebration of marriage, and in the normal course of events a man such as Dimitri Kouvaris would have wanted an almighty splash—with his aunt there, of course, and all the distant relatives Irini had spoken of, his large circle of friends and business colleagues, the press, all in admiring awestruck attendance.

Useless to confront him with what she knew—because with the heir he wanted so badly now on the horizon he would deny everything until his face turned blue. There was too much at stake for him to do anything else.

So for the next few weeks she would play it his way. Grit her teeth and fall in with the charade of starting their marriage afresh. There was too much at stake for her to do anything other. Oh, how she wished she'd come straight out with it on the night of that party—insisted that Irini repeated what she'd said in front of Dimitri. On the face of it Amanda's advice had seemed sensible after all, she was married to a well-heeled Greek herself and would know how their minds ticked. But, oh, how she wished she hadn't taken it!

She would have to find a way to warn her parents that their comfortable new lifestyle would soon be a thing of the past, give them time to make contingency plans. And plan her own bid for freedom—because no way was he going to take her baby from her.

If she couldn't bear the thought of giving up the tiny life inside her now, she couldn't begin to contemplate how very much worse it would be after the birth.

When they were back on the mainland she would be able to work on what she had to do. Transfer some of what she had always considered to be the over-the-top personal allowance he'd made her from Greece into her still open but paltry account back in England for starters.

Not that she wanted anything from him for herself. She definitely didn't, and the thought of actually doing it turned her stomach, but for her baby's sake she had to have some funds behind her. Enough to live frugally until the birth, until she could rebuild her career and work to keep them both.

And back in England she wouldn't make the unthinking mistake she'd made before. She wouldn't go near her family, but hide somewhere he'd never find her.

In the meantime she would bide her time, let him think she was willing to make a fresh start. It was the only way she could ensure that he didn't suspect what she was planning. Besides, pulling the wool over his eyes while playing him at his own game was one way of paying him back for what he had done. Taken her heart and broken it.

She left the room and went down to find him, her head high, the welcome upsurge of renewed self-confidence momentarily smothering the pain of what was happening. It lasted until she tracked him down, hearing his voice, the tone low and warmly intimate, issuing from what turned out to be the huge airy kitchen. That upsurge of self-confidence drained away as he abruptly ended a call as soon as she entered the room, closing down his mobile and slipping it into his back pocket.

'Maddie—'

'Dimitri—' How she kept her voice cool, her smile pleasant, she would never know. He looked—what? Guilty? Glittering golden eyes, a faint band of colour across those sculpted cheekbones.

'You look so much better. Pregnancy suits you!'

'Does it? That's nice.' She wandered further into the room. He'd been working at the huge central table, but the much smaller one beneath one of the open windows had been laid. Plates, a bowl of crisp salad, rolls, cold chicken and a ham.

The way he'd ended what had obviously been a highly personal conversation, judging by his intimate tone, the spattering of endearments she'd recognised in his native tongue, the call ending so abruptly at her approach, made the hairs on the back of her neck stand up on end.

'Who were you talking to?' She was making like a suspicious wife—but who could blame her in the dire circumstances she found herself in? 'Irini, was it?' Couldn't wait to tell her the good news?'

She watched his features harden, the softness in his eyes replaced by an unhidden glint of cold anger. Noted that he didn't answer her specific question directly. 'I'll never understand what you've got against her,' he stated in a cool challenge. 'Whenever she's around you show all your prickles, close down, and when she tries to speak to you you answer in monosyllables. It upsets her. She would like to be your friend. And believe me, Maddie, she needs friends.'

So protective of the woman he loved. Her cheeks burning, she could have ripped her tongue out. She would have to watch what she said in future, especially when it concerned that woman!

She could tell him exactly what she held against Irini. Starting with that hateful conversation at that first party, when she'd told her her days as Dimitri's wife were numbered, and why. But doing so now would put

him on his guard, put her plans to leave him in
jeopardy. Unfortunately, the time for coming out into
the open was past.

So she simply shrugged, essayed a smile, and told
him, 'Sorry, I'll try harder. She's just not my cup of tea,
and we've nothing in common. But, I don't think we
should quarrel about it, do you?'

Dimitri expelled a slow breath. He felt something warm
enfold his heart, banish irritation. Did she know how
adorable she looked? How the band of freckles across her
pretty nose moved him to an unbearable tenderness? An
almost painful hunger gripped him in a vice as he met
those clear blue fathomless eyes, his heart turning over and
swelling within him. Maddie, his wife, was carrying his
child. Nothing would put that child at risk.

Nothing! For the sake of his child, for his child's
future happiness and security, with two parents in
apparent harmony with each other, he would wipe her
rejection of him from his mind. Forget it. Try to make
their marriage work. And to do that, to forget what she
had done and why, it must never be spoken of. That he
was determined on.

He extended his hand towards her. 'Come and eat.'
He waited, his shoulders relaxing when, after a tension-
filled moment, she gave him her hand. A ghost of a
frown darkened his brow as, slightly ahead of her, he led
her towards the small table beneath the window. It
seemed as though she was falling in with his earlier
stated wishes. Making a fresh start, burying the past,
wiping the word *divorce* from her vocabulary.

Why? Should it matter? He knew his reasons, knew
they were sound. Was the news of her pregnancy her

reason? Had it settled her, made her earlier behaviour appear as the nonsense it was? Or had his promise that she would want for nothing, that whatever her heart desired would be hers, been the deciding factor?

The former, he devoutly hoped. Until she'd left him for no good reason that he'd been able to come up with apart from a fat divorce settlement, he would have said she didn't possess an avaricious bone in her body. And yet how could he know what went on inside that lovely head of hers?

The time was past when he could have done what he'd brought her here to do—insist that she reveal her true motivations behind her desire for a divorce. Such an insistence would be counter-productive in the new regime he'd set up. No arguments about that!

No looking back.

Slate wiped clean.

Fresh start.

Seeing her seated, he helped her to a little of everything on the table, slid the plate in front of her and sat opposite, his own appetite—roused and ravaging after the news that he was to be a father—completely gone. Was it pride that kept him from acknowledging that he wanted her to stay with him, make their marriage work, because he was important to her?

He refused to dwell on that possibility. She had wronged him, shamed him, but he was now prepared to overlook that. And whatever her reasons for her seeming compliance to his wishes it was a step in the right direction—a step towards what he must have: a stable relationship for the sake of their unborn child.

He had endured a cold and loveless childhood following the deaths of his parents when he'd been too young to properly remember them, so he was determined that his child would be surrounded by the permanence of parental love.

And no way would a child of his suffer the trauma of a broken home, a marriage gone wrong, with all the attendant recriminations and back-biting, the divided loyalties that would torment any child shunted between two bitter parents.

Watching her eat a little of the food and push the remainder around her plate, he wondered how far her compliance with his wishes would take her.

As far as the marriage bed?

And did he really want that?

The answer, he knew, to his annoyance, was yes. Despite her past behaviour, the shaming of his honour, he wanted her. Even more than when he'd first encountered her in Cristos's courtyard.

And that was saying something!

CHAPTER EIGHT

DIMITRI rose from the table as if propelled by a rocket, pushed back his chair and, sounding almost painfully polite, said, 'You must rest this afternoon, Maddie. I insist. It has been a traumatic morning.' One dark brow elevated as she stubbornly remained seated. His mouth flattened. 'Come, I will see you to your room.'

Leaving her barely touched meal, Maddie got to her feet with extreme reluctance. An hour or two of solitude, the opportunity to at least try to relax and consider her situation calmly, had its glaringly obvious advantages. But, perversely, she didn't want to give him the satisfaction of seeing her meekly fall in with all his orders. He had managed to demean her until she felt lower than the ground she walked on. Was she to have no pride left whatsoever?

Suddenly her legs felt horribly unsteady. He was spot-on about this morning's trauma. And every bit of it was his fault!

It had started with his humiliation of her and come to a dramatic crescendo with the news of her pregnancy. So a short rest, the brief and blessed oblivion of sleep, seemed like the best idea she'd heard in a long while.

And if he smugly assumed she was falling in with his wishes it couldn't be helped.

'I'm sure I will be all right on my own,' she was forced to point out, not wanting him anywhere near her, because he was no longer her dearest love, he was her enemy. Her pregnancy had rammed that reality home as nothing else could have done. Muttering vociferously, he ignored her statement of independence, swept her up into his arms and headed for the staircase.

'Put me down! I'm not an invalid! I can manage!'

'I'm sure you can. But while I am with you, you don't have to.'

He knew he sounded cold. Could do nothing about it. He could barely trust himself to speak. Watching her across that table, he'd been hit by the usual upsurge of savage hunger that always afflicted him in her presence—had done ever since he'd first set eyes on her for the first time. The wanting was strong enough to cause actual physical hurt, leading inevitably to the thought of the marriage bed.

But he knew that resuming those mind-shattering pleasures was out of the question until things were calmer between them and he could begin to forgive himself for the earlier humiliation he'd dealt her, which now severely appalled him.

Whatever her reasons for wanting out of their marriage—and he no longer wished to know them because the future was all that mattered—she didn't deserve that type of treatment.

He hoisted her body closer to the hard strength of his and effortlessly mounted the stairs, while Maddie desperately tried to stop the tears that stung the back of her eyes from falling. Held this close to him, to the man she had adored with everything in her, was torture. Worse than torture. Because her body was letting her down again, responding wholeheartedly to him even as what little was left of her brain told her all she wanted to do was punch him!

Wicked, treacherous heat flared deep inside her as he shouldered through the door to the master bedroom and slid her to her feet at the side of the massive bed. He was still so close, too close. He was so magnificent, so unfairly sexy, full of careless masculinity. It was as if his body was a silent call to her—a call which drew an immediate response from her soul, from a loving heart her logical mind was unable to control.

Maddie turned swiftly, caught between the edge of the bed and his superbly powerful frame. A smothered sob snagged her throat as blistering heat gathered deep inside her and made her heart flip over.

She despised herself for her body's unmanageable response to him. She knew what he was. Cruel enough to make her love him and then toss that love back in her face as if it were something of no value whatsoever. So why did she crave him like a forbidden drug? She would never have described herself as weak, lacking will power, but she obviously was, and the knowledge flayed her.

As if sensing her distress, he stepped away from her, his strong jaw set, golden eyes uncompromisingly grim as he told her, 'Rest now. I shall be working in the study at the far end of the old wing should you need me. And, Maddie—' His voice faltered momentarily, then incised on. 'Please accept my apologies for my earlier despicable behaviour. Such a thing will never happen again,

I promise on my life. I quite understand why you felt the need to run from the house. From me.'

Turning with his inherent grace, he left the room. Stunned, Maddie plopped down on the bed and just sat there. Shaking.

The arrogant, domineering Greek male had actually apologised! The moon must have turned blue and she hadn't noticed!

Unused to putting a foot wrong in his world-spanning business dealings, or in his relationships with friends and colleagues, he had actually admitted being in the wrong. Why? Unaccustomed humility? Or an integral part of his cynical kiss-and-make-up scenario?

But there wouldn't be any kissing, would there?

She was safely pregnant. There was no longer any need for him to grit his teeth, take her to bed and think of Irini!

Curling up on the tumbled sheets, she buried her face in a pillow and eventually fell into an uneasy sleep, wondering why that obvious conclusion didn't bring her the deep relief it should.

It was cooler when she woke. The searing midday heat had been replaced by a soft, balmy warmth that drifted through the open windows, fluttering the delicate muslin drapes. Her eyes felt gritty, her mouth parched, her brain fuzzy. She would have to freshen up, she decided vaguely. Get out of the dress she'd fallen asleep in, move herself. Then the hateful reality of her situation hit her like a sledgehammer and enfolded her.

Staunchly telling herself that she was going to have to get used to it or lose her sanity, she firmed her soft mouth and swung her feet to the floor, her eyes lighting on the jug of orange juice and the single tall crystal glass on the bedside table.

Dimitri? Had to be. Schooling the sudden and unwelcome mush out of her heart and replacing it with cold reality was easy. He hadn't provided the freshly squeezed juice because he cared about *her.* He cared about the welfare of the coming baby. He would cosset her, wrap her in cotton wool until her child was born. Then get rid of her.

She would take his plans and reduce them to ashes. Even if it did mean having to grit her teeth and play him at his own devious game for a few more weeks.

She hated him! Nevertheless, she poured and drank gratefully, noting that the ice cubes hadn't begun to melt. So he must have come to the room in the past few minutes. Was that what had woken her? Was she that aware of him, attuned to him, even in sleep?

It was a shattering thought. She didn't want it to be like that. She had to learn to be indifferent to him. Had to.

Starting with doing her own thing.

Hoping he'd gone back to his study and intended to stay there, she stripped off the now crumpled and wilted sundress she'd put on for the doctor's arrival and got into a sleek white one-piece swimsuit, bemoaning the fact that, sleek as it might be, it did nothing to disguise the curve of her breasts and well-rounded hips.

Not for the first time she wondered how he could have brought himself to make love to her, preferring, as he obviously did, the ultra-sophisticated stick-insect type such as his beloved Irini.

Dimitri had mentioned a swimming pool, so she was going to find it and enjoy the cool waters and continue the long haul of not only acting but actually *being* indifferent to him. To knock firmly on the head the sneaky wish that her husband truly loved her, only her, and that their time here in romantic seclusion really was a belated honeymoon.

In a hollow beyond a sweeping stone terrace lay the immense oval pool, surrounded by slender cypress trees, blue water lazy, limpid, inviting.

The gentle breeze caressed her exposed skin, carrying the scents of sea, dried grasses and aromatic herbs. Dropping the fluffy jade-green towel she'd brought with her onto the cool marble surround, Maddie took a deep breath and dived in at the deep end, determined to forget her situation and the shameful fact that she'd been too stupid to smell a rat when the super-eligible Dimitri Kouvaris, charismatic and absolutely gorgeous, and a millionaire many times over, had proposed marriage to an insignificant grubber-around-in-the-soil-nobody like her, after such a remarkably short acquaintance.

She would relax, do a few gentle lengths, empty her mind to everything but the perfection of the early evening, the soft caress of the water, and find tranquility—because bad thoughts and a brain that was in knots couldn't be good for the baby inside her.

And she was doing just fine in that respect when a splash at the opposite end of the pool, the deep end, had her feet finding the bottom in a flurry, her eyes widening, sparking blue fire, as Dimitri scythed through the water towards her in a powerful crawl.

Did he have to spoil everything? Even her relaxing half hour in the swimming pool—not to mention her whole life!

With water lapping her waist she was too stricken to move until he got close. Then, galvanised, she hauled herself out of the pool in a shower of water droplets and headed like a bullet to where she'd left the towel.

But he was there before her, blocking her way. Thankfully, she was able to keep her instinctive groan internal as his honeyed drawl sent shivers right down to her toes. She wanted to drag her eyes from him but couldn't as he said, 'Slow down! Honeymoons on secluded Greek islands are meant to be slow and lazy. Relaxed. I will help you to learn that much.'

Her toes curled in reaction to his nearness, to the bronzed body glistening with moisture, tempting her to touch and go on touching, to slide her hands over the muscular strength of his chest, the skin like oiled silk and just as sensuous. Her fingers would glide lower, over the washboard-flat stomach, to the top of the black briefs that did nothing at all to modestly disguise his manhood—

Smartly clasping her hands behind her back to stop them straying of their own volition, she countered on a rasp of breath, and with no pretence of the rapprochement he'd earlier suggested, 'I was perfectly relaxed until you showed up!'

She bent to retrieve the towel and cover herself up, because he was no one's fool and would have no trouble working out why her wretched breasts were pushing at the clinging fabric of her swimsuit as if hedonistically eager for the touch of his hands, his mouth.

But he stayed her before she could reach her objective, strong, finely made hands on her shoulders as he brought her upright, moving in closer as he reminded her grittily, 'I am not your enemy. I am your husband. And I want you so much it hurts.'

Shaken by that admission, she allowed her eyes to meet his. His hands on her naked shoulders sent electrifying shivers down her spine. His eyes were hot gold, burning into her where they touched—her shamefully peaking breasts, the quivering curve of her tummy, and lower, making her shift her feet, part her thighs with blatant invitation and no conscious thought whatsoever.

She jerked in a ragged breath as his hands slid slowly down from her shoulders to fasten around her slender waist and pull her with aching deliberation against him. He hadn't been lying, was her almost incoherent thought. The state of his arousal left her in no doubt as to the truth of his gritty statement.

Unable to decide what she was thinking, she felt terrifyingly vulnerable, torn between the conflicting need to distance herself from him in every way there was and wanting her charismatic, once-adored husband just as much as she ever had.

The deed was done. She was pregnant. So why should he still want her sexually? She had expected a spurious kindness—not for her sake, but for his child's. But this? 'We are not enemies. What we once had was beautiful. We can and will reclaim it,' Dimitri reiterated rawly. 'Between us we have made a baby, have created a new life. The future can be golden, *chrysi mou*, if you will let it be. You still want me—as I need you—I am ready and willing to forget the immediate past, and I hope you are, too.'

A gentle hand slid up behind her head, long fingers slipping through her bright hair, lifting her face, her mouth, to the seductive invasion of a kiss that proved his point—because she could not resist the hunger of his lips, the tongue that dipped, teased and tormented until she was writhing against him, heart hammering, veins running with liquid fire.

Everything inside her quivered as with one fluid movement he lifted her in his arms and carried her to the bedroom, his mouth unceasing in its ravishment of hers until he laid her on the bed and came down beside her, divesting them both of damp garments in the time it took to draw breath.

She had expected immediate consummation, indeed her body craved it, but he whispered, 'Slowly, my sweet, slowly,' which she translated as *Gently, for our baby's sake*. But then she didn't care, because the wicked expertise of his sensual mouth, his knowing hands, as he brought every inch of her restlessly writhing body to a wild crescendo of excitement drove everything else out of her mind until at last, responding to her moans of 'Please—Dimitri, please!' he sank between her thighs and with one long thrust instigated an unstoppable storm of white-hot passion that spiralled until control splintered and was lost in the primitive rhythm that swept her up and beyond the very pinnacle of ecstasy.

Held in his arms, his fantastic body melded to the yielding softness of hers, Maddie floated gently back to earth, loving the way he dropped tiny kisses on her damp forehead, the tip of her small nose, the corner of her mouth, revelling in sweet satiation until, at the unmistakable hardening of his body, he released her with a shaky laugh, a reluctant, 'I am too greedy for you! I hadn't meant this to happen.

But you, alone among women, are too much temptation for me!'

He sprang off the bed, telling her after a rapid glance at the watch that adorned his flat wrist, 'Xanthe will arrive at any moment with the evening meal she has prepared.' Slanting her a smile he promised, his stunning eyes filled with dancing golden lights, 'I will be patient until after we have eaten,' and strode to the bathroom where, above the sound of the shower, she could hear him singing in the tuneful baritone she had once delighted to hear.

Pleased with himself, she thought sourly, as bleak despair again settled around her, a too-regular visitor, and as demeaning as it was unwelcome. So he had a highly over-active libido. He could have sex with her while loving another woman. No problem when his eager wife was so obviously more than willing to participate.

And as for her—well, she was deeply ashamed of herself. Telling herself that sexual desire—lust, if you like—had the habit of taking over, crippling the mind, filling the body and heating the blood to boiling point, did nothing to excuse what she had done.

Her body aching from his intimate possession, she waited, scrambling a sheet around her nakedness. At one time nothing would have prevented her from joining him in the shower, delighting in the welcome she knew he would give her as they teased each other with soap-slicked, deliciously tormenting hands, laughter dissolving into the ecstasy of out-of-this-world passion.

Now, nothing would make her join him in there. And so she waited, subduing the sob of self-loathing that was burning her lungs, compressing her lips to stop her soft, kiss-swollen mouth from trembling, until he emerged from the *en suite* bathroom, towel-drying his thick dark hair, his smile something else as he imparted, 'I heard the quad bike arriving.' His smile widened to a grin. 'Yiannis will have nothing to do with it, but Xanthe uses it at every opportunity—flat out!'

Unable to respond for her swamping awareness of that naked, lithely lean and powerful physique, Maddie willed her pulses to stop racing, waiting until he had rapidly clothed himself in narrow white jeans topped by a silky black shirt, open-necked, sleeves rolled up to display tanned, muscular forearms, before getting out, 'I would like to phone my parents.'

She marvelled at his duplicity as he reached his mobile from the top of a dressing chest, found the number, and passed the instrument to her, saying, 'Of course—you'll want to tell them our good news. I know they'll be delighted to hear they can look forward to being grandparents again. Be sure to give them my regards.' A swift kiss landed on her brow. 'Don't be too long. I'd speak to them myself, but I must see to Xanthe. We'll eat on the terrace and count the stars as they come out to celebrate our new beginning.'

And he was gone, leaving her listening to the ringing tone and fuming. Give them his regards—oh, the low-life! How could he? When all the time he was doubt-lessly planning on throwing them off his property when he no longer had need of his disposable wife!

She had to warn them of that strong possibility.

But how to do it gently, without creating panic and outraged anxiety, when her mother's bubbly conversa-tion was filled with enthusiasm for the farmhouse they had recently moved into, her redecorating plans, the imminent arrival of the new glasshouse, and the hard work her menfolk were putting in? 'No, not your father,' she said soothingly. 'He is being sensible. He takes gentle exercise each day and contents himself with keeping the accounts.'

Eventually Maddie slid in a question—when her mother drew breath after happily imparting the fact that the old fellow hadn't farmed intensively for a decade, merely keeping a flock of sheep and a few free-range hens and pigs, so the land wasn't contaminated with nasty chemicals—'Did Dad go over the small print of the lease for the farmhouse and land?' And fingers crossed, but without too much hope, 'There *is* a properly drawn-up lease?'

Ringing silence greeted the question that had stopped the flow of excited information in its tracks. Maddie felt truly dreadful.

Was poor old Mum belatedly recalling that Dad had failed to check the details of his contract of employment when the men in suits had taken over the estate? Maddie hated having to do this to her family, and her heart plummeted even further when Joan Ryan asked with some bewilderment, 'What lease?'

So nothing had been put in writing concerning her family's security of tenure. Even though Maddie had known what would happen, having the fact thrust under her nose reminded her much too forcefully of Dimitri's threats, and made her feel dreadfully nauseous.

Until her mother questioned, 'Didn't Dimitri tell you? No, I suppose he wouldn't. He's too big-hearted to boast about his generosity! He bought the property, but it's in my and your father's name. We *own* it,

Maddie. We did feel a bit awkward about it—poor but proud, as your Dad always says! He tried to persuade your Dimitri to make it a capital loan, but he was having none of it. We were family, he said, and the cash outlay was peanuts to him. You married a man in a million!' This was followed by a slightly anxious, 'Everything's still all right between you? We were worried. On the face of it, Dimitri's everything a parent could want for a daughter. But—'

Her head reeling from what she'd heard, Maddie put in, 'We're fine, Mum.' And, because they had to know, 'I'm pregnant.'

No need to worry them now. It would be a few more weeks before she had to tell them the truth. She was more than happy to listen to her mother's overjoyed exclamations as her mind spun, trying to make sense of this new information.

CHAPTER NINE

AFTER the call ended Maddie stood immobile under the shower, her brow furrowed, as she grappled with Joan Ryan's revelations, and what they meant.

Thanks to Dimitri's generosity her parents' home and livelihood were safe. There was, of course, huge relief because from the start he had led her to believe that her family would be out of their new home and business like a shot if she didn't toe the line and stick with their marriage—but the question remained.

Why? Why had he done that?

To force her to resume her marital duties? Share his bed until the child he needed was conceived.

Obvious.

And yet...

That kind of thoughtful generosity didn't gel with the kind of guy she had categorised him as being—a heartless blackmailer who would use any means to get what he wanted and suffer not one pang of conscience when he made her family face real hardship when he'd got it, because they were unimportant, mere peasants. He didn't fit that box now.

It looked as if he were the kind of guy who would

spend vast amounts of money setting her parents up in their own home and business, generously sorting out the difficulties they were facing and were financially and emotionally unable to cope with.

In the situation that had faced her parents any other needle-sharp, super-wealthy businessman with a philanthropic streak a mile wide might have done what he had done, she conceded, but he would have kept the deeds in his name, as an investment, one among many.

But Dimitri had gone one huge stride further. His generosity shook her, made her acknowledge that he wasn't all as bad as she had named him. Far from it.

Could she have misjudged him in other aspects of their relationship?

Irini?

The attention he lavished on the other woman when she was around—which had always been far too often for Maddie's liking—could be explained away by the fact that his aunt had counted her as one of the family from the time of her birth. And the relationship had rubbed off because for Dimtri family was all important.

Having lost both his parents at an early age, he was determined to create a family of his own. She could understand that because he would lavish care on anyone he considered part of his family, as witness how he had helped his parents-by-marriage.

But she couldn't explain away that overheard telephone conversation when he had confirmed his love for the beautiful Greek woman, dropped everything and shot off to be with her. Nothing could. Or the way the two of them had vanished together during the week before he'd brought her here to this island. And, although he hadn't confirmed it—or denied it either, come to that—the intimate-sounding phone call she'd interrupted had to have been to Irini, breaking the news of the pregnancy they had both waited so anxiously for.

And Irini's spiteful warning on the night of that party, spelling out exactly why the man who was probably the most eligible bachelor in the whole of Greece had chosen to marry an insignificant nobody like her, was solid, irrefutable fact.

Her mind preoccupied, Maddie dressed and went down to find him, uselessly wishing yet again that she had never taken Amanda's advice and kept quiet about Irini's warning, sticking her head in the sand and putting it down to the malicious spite of a jealous woman.

Her pride had stopped her flinging what she knew and what she strongly suspected at him after he had flown to England to find her and force her to return to him. And now, it seemed, it was too late.

He had categorically stated that he no longer wished to know why she had left him. He wouldn't listen and, knowing him, his masculine pride, she could understand why. In leaving him, demanding a divorce, she had rejected him and all that he was. His ego wouldn't let him listen to why she had done it. Not if he wanted them to start over, wipe the slate clean. Make the marriage work.

Until the safe delivery of their child?

'We'll stop here. You mustn't overtire yourself.' A couple of days ago she had accused him of wrapping her in cotton wool. True, he conceded with a wry twist of his mouth. He simply couldn't help himself. He took this pregnancy seriously, and his part in it was to cherish her.

Dimitri slid the strap of the picnic bag off one broad shoulder as they reached one of his favourite spots on the island. A gentle green hollow beside an abundant freshwater spring, shaded from the burning sun by a grove of ancient, long-neglected olive trees.

Golden eyes soft and slightly narrowed between thick black lashes, he watched her wander over the lush green grass, down to where the water bubbled into a natural stone basin. The gauzy cotton skirt she was wearing, in shades of primrose, pale blue and cream moved against the lovely legs that had acquired a healthy tan over the week they had spent here. He adored looking at her. He only had to look at her to want her.

Their time here together during this past week had been perfect. Their marriage was back on track.

Or almost.

Swimming in the pool or in the gentle waters of one of the small bays, exploring the island and the dozens of tiny beaches, lazy afternoons and languid evenings, hot sex—everything was pointing to her willingness to put the recent past behind them, to make a fresh start, as he had wanted, for the sake of the coming child.

Except...

He missed her once-ready, infectious laughter. Had caught the wistful look in those clear blue eyes, quickly extinguished when his eyes connected with hers. But it was there, all the same, in his memory.

It troubled him. But no way was he prepared to question her.

Because he wouldn't like the answer?

The thought came unbidden. She'd wanted a divorce. Since the news of her pregnancy there was no chance of that. And even if he strongly suspected her reasons, he would have to live with those suspicions and do his damnedest to disregard them. If she'd wanted her freedom with the financial cushion of a hefty slice of alimony he didn't want to hear her confess it, not now!

He'd said they were to make a fresh start, wipe the slate clean. Every child had a right to a close, loving family, the care of both parents, and he had a duty to provide it.

And that was how it was going to be. His decision. End of story. Their future and that of the coming child was all that mattered—unsullied by a knowledge he didn't want to have.

Thrusting the unwelcome and rare bout of introspection out of his head, he strode towards her. She was kneeling by the spring, her hands gliding slowly back and forth in the cool clear water. As he reached her she glanced up at him from beneath the wide brim of the straw hat he insisted she wear and smiled. Her smile touched his heart, turned it over. It always did.

'It's lovely! So cool!'

His heart twisted, the breath in his lungs tightening. The band of freckles across her neat little nose was more pronounced, and perspiration dewed her short upper lip. The blue of her eyes between those thick fringing lashes was clear and perfect. She was the loveliest thing he had ever seen.

Leaning forward, she cupped her hands in the water and sluiced it over her face in one graceful movement, then rose to her feet, gasping just a little as her hat tumbled off her head.

Her skin glistened. Droplets trickled onto the soft,

tempting skin between firm breasts that were partly exposed by the buttons she'd undone at the front of the sleeveless, cream-coloured fine cotton cropped top she was wearing. With him she was so uninhibited, her sexuality so natural. It blew his mind.

Instinctively, his hands went to her upper arms to steady her. He heard the tiny huff of expelled breath as her soft lips parted at his touch, felt the inevitable answering excitement tighten his body.

Those soft, full lips promised passion—the spectacular passion that neither of them could deny. He bent his head and touched them with his own, revelled in her immediate response. Driven as he always was with her, he parted his mouth from hers, going lower, to capture the crystal droplets that sparkled between her breasts. His hands followed. Hands and mouth.

His hunger for her was as intense as ever, but, mindful of the tiny life inside her, he was now more than ordinarily gentle as he lowered her to the cool green earth. Ignoring the way her body arched impatiently into his, he slowly removed her clothing, the fever grew in her beautiful eyes as fine tremors of tension rippled over her gorgeous nakedness when his hands, a whisper of motion, moved over her engorged, divine breasts, down over the slight curve of her tummy to rest, trembling now, on the springy nest of curls between her parted thighs.

He heard her near-desperate sigh of need just as he felt control slip away from him, and he breathed her name, thrusting with as much tenderness as he could find deep inside her as she wrapped her legs around his narrow hips in eager welcome.

* * *

Later—how much later Maddie neither knew nor cared—Dimitri moved in her arms, his own arms releasing her, the smile he gave her soft and satisfied. Precisely mirroring her own, she guessed.

It was always like this for them. They only had to touch each other and hot passion, driven need took over, Maddie dreamily acknowledged as he got to his feet, locating his stone-coloured chinos and getting into them with the economy of movement that was so much a part of him.

'We forgot the picnic. Xanthe will be irredeemably upset if we take it back untouched.' Humour warmed his fantastic amber eyes as they caressed her flushed features. 'Get dressed, *chrysi mou*, while I sort it out.'

Hoisting herself up on one elbow, the lush grass cool beneath her naked body, the slight breeze from the sea caressing her skin, she watched him move away to the lip of the green hollow where he had left the picnic bag Xanthe had filled for them this morning, missing his physical closeness already.

A too-familiar ache took possession of the region around her heart. His absence from her side, short-lived though it was, still felt like a pain.

When she was with him, close, talking, swimming, lazily exploring the island, touching, hands clasped, fingers entwined she could forget—lose herself in the wonder of him, even convince herself that he wanted a happy, stable marriage as much as she did, that she came first with him and always would.

And their frequent lovemaking had nothing to do with primal animal lust. At least to her it always seemed so. There was passion, yes, but tenderness too, a feeling of closeness, of a bond of deep love that couldn't be broken.

And yet…

Separated from him, even for a short while, at such a small physical distance, as she was now, she felt the doubts return, chilling her, eating into her. And the searing near-unbearable sorrow.

At the start of this week she had made up her mind to go along with his fresh-start dictate, because that would put him off guard, make it much easier for her to bring her plans to fruition, to make her bid for freedom when they returned to Athens and put herself and her coming baby right out of his and Irini's reach.

And now she knew that whatever she did her family's home and livelihood were safe, there was not a single thing to stop her.

But every hour that passed had made her hate that decision, despise herself for reaching it. It had been made with her head, but her heart had swiftly overruled her brain, leading her to fall ever more deeply in love with him, wanting, needing, to be with him always.

The thought of leaving him broke her heart.

Aware that Dimitri had almost finished laying out the food he'd taken from the cooler-bag on the vivid scarlet cloth Xanthe had provided, Maddie pulled herself together and hurried into her discarded clothing.

And made her mind up.

Despite his firmly stated order that they were to forget she'd ever wanted to end their marriage and were never to speak of it, she was going to have to. Would tell him exactly what Irini had told her. He would, in any case, staunchly deny it, in view of her pregnancy. That was more than a strong possibility. But at least he would know the truth of what had lain behind her headlong flight from him and their marriage. She owed herself that much.

'Come, slowcoach! Remember our baby is hungry, even if you are not!'

That slow, magical smile of his made her poor heart flip over. He had straightened, was standing tall and proud now, hands on his narrow hips, bare feet planted firmly, a little apart, on the sun-warmed sparse grass at the top of the bank. He was shirtless, his magnificent upper body exposed, his skin sleek, tanned olive by the Greek sun. Much too touchable.

As usual his sexuality disorientated her, but her eyes shadowed as she walked towards him, and she knew she had to be strong and tell him the truth. But feed it in gradually, at the right opportunity. That way maybe she'd get the truth from him.

Blurting it out like a bolshie teenager might release the knot of tension that coiled painfully inside her whenever she thought of what Irini had told her, of his aunt's unpleasant comments about her gross unsuitability as a bride for her high-status nephew, remembered the tone of his voice as he'd assured the other woman that he loved her.

Yes, getting it off her chest, where it festered, out into the open, might release that tension. But hurl the accusation at him and he'd instinctively and immediately deny it.

She had to be more subtle than that.

That look was back in her eyes again, Dimitri noted, his own brows lowering in response as she sank onto the ground beside the lavish spread. Perhaps time and patience on his part would remove it. The thing to do, he assured himself firmly, was to concentrate on the positive side of their marriage. Forget everything else.

'How long can we stay here?' Even to her own ears her voice sounded overly-bright, she decided helplessly as she obeyed his hand gesture and helped herself to one of Xanthe's delicious stuffed vine leaves.

'Bored already?' Lightly said, but the thread of anxiety was there. He deplored it.

'Not at all. Just interested. It's so lovely here.' The morsel eaten, she reached for a tiny cheese pastry, not looking at him until he told her, 'Another two weeks, *pethi mou*, and then back to Athens to get the refurbishment of the nursery wing in hand, and get you to a top-notch gynaecologist. Sound good?'

Glancing at him then, she ached with love for him, felt an onslaught of longing that was frightening in its intensity. He was so compelling, so beautiful. The hard, tanned planes of his sculpted features, the soft sable hair, the sensual line of the mouth that promised and delivered heaven, the warm golden eyes.

The ache intensified. Two more weeks of ecstatic self-delusion and then…

Reaching forward, he opened a flask and filled two glasses, telling her, 'There are lemon trees here. Yiannis tends them and sells the ripe fruit on the mainland. And Xanthe makes the best lemonade you will ever have tasted.' He handed a glass to her and tipped his own against it. 'A toast. To our baby—may he or she live long and happy and much loved!'

Her eyes misting as the delicious chilled liquid slid down her parched throat, Maddie thought, He *does* want our child, more than anything. The only contentious issue was why.

He confirmed it when he told her smokily, 'I am filled with delight at the thought of the child you will give me, my Maddie.' Almost reverently he laid a hand on her tummy, surprising her with his words. 'Before our marriage we spoke of our desire for children, do you remember?'

Maddie dipped her head in silent acknowledgement. Not answering vocally because her throat had tightened too much to allow her to speak. Not looking at him, although she could feel his eyes on her.

Of course she remembered! He had been at pains to make sure she wanted his baby before the actual low-key ceremony because that had been the whole point of the exercise, hadn't it? And, gullible sucker that she'd been then, her head spinning at the way he'd romanced her, swept her off her usually firmly-grounded feet, she'd given him the answer he'd been looking for. Of course she wanted children—his children. The more the merrier!

If she'd turned round and told him that, no, she didn't want motherhood for at least ten years—if then, if ever—the wedding would never have taken place. He would have disappeared in a puff of smoke! Would it have happened that way? Dear God, she hoped not! But how could she know?

Then further confounded her when he said, with a sincerity she could not doubt, 'I confess I would like more than one child, but it's not a burning issue. Growing up, I missed my parents, wished they were still alive, wished I had brothers and sisters, a close family.'

Naked, powerful, sun-kissed shoulders lifted in a wry shrug. 'I guess that explains why I would like a whole gang of them!' His eyes held hers—soft eyes, soft mouth, soft smile. 'But I promise you, *chrysi mou*, there is no pressure. I might desire to give you at least three babies, but it will be for you and you alone to decide. If you decide that one pregnancy is enough for you, then he or she will be enough for me, too. This I promise.'

CHAPTER TEN

FOR several moments Maddie was silent. Her brain had gone numb. She couldn't think of a single thing to say. At least nothing that would verbalise her muddled feelings in any way that made some sort of sense.

Then, deep blue eyes wide and uncomprehending, she got out, 'Do you really mean that?'

If he did, it altered everything. In her favour? She was unsure of that. A puzzled frown appeared between her eyes. On the one hand her whole body tingled with the electric sting of unsquashable hope, while on the other suspicion of his motives made her heart shrivel.

'Of course I mean it!' Lean bronzed fingers brushed her tumbling fringe aside, gently caressing away the tiny frown line. 'Every word. It is for you to decide how large our family grows or how small it stays. What you wish is my wish too, my Maddie.'

The way he said her name made her heart turn over. As if it were spoken with devotion.

Devotion?

She might be a self-confessed hopeless sucker when he turned on the charm, but she really couldn't let herself believe that!

Once she had believed it with all her heart and soul. True, he had never actually said he loved her but she had truly believed he did. But everything was different now. Painfully, horribly different. And she would be a fool to forget it, to let herself be carried away by the prospect of paradise—the true and loving marriage he appeared to be offering.

But those brilliant dark-lashed eyes were mesmerising her. For the life of her she couldn't look away, even though she knew that every look, every soft word, might be hiding the harsh and ugly truth.

Unconsciously, she shook her head. 'And if I said I wanted you to give me at least six babies…' Her voice tailed off on an intake of breath at the enormity of her weak and instinctive compliance in his—his what?— Manipulation?

He smiled that slow, melting smile of his. 'Then I would rejoice in your maternal if excessive desire! But I would, I think, gently persuade you to consider three a happy number. I could not stand by and see you exhaust yourself by producing the beginnings of a football team! You are far too precious to me.'

The tips of his fingers trailed lightly from her cheekbones down to the side of her jaw. Maddie closed her eyes, lost in his touch. So gentle, so caring, so achingly seductive.

The trouble with loving someone as much as she loved Dimitri was the way you wanted to believe everything he said—clung onto it because it gave you hope, conveniently forgetting everything else, she thought to herself, appalled by the weak stupidity she seemed incapable of kicking into touch.

Her mouth dry, her heart thumping heavily, she steeled herself to broach the subject of his mistress. She couldn't afford to be confrontational, she knew that. An open attack on his motives—his downright wickedness—would only serve to elicit an immediate and vehement denial.

Aiming for a light, only vaguely interested tone, she made herself relax back against the arm he held around her waist, leaning into him, and ventured, 'I believe Irini is unable to have children?' She waited, feeling downright nauseous, for the telltale and instinctive tightening of his body that would tell her that her words had put him on his guard.

It didn't come as he bent his head to rest it against hers and confirmed, sounding completely relaxed and unfazed about it, 'No. An accident when she was a child.' She felt his minimal shrug. 'But it's not the tragedy it would be for most women, believe me. Irini has a positive aversion to children; she can't stand to be around them. There's not one maternal bone in her body, so her infertility is for the best in my opinion. Children need love more than anything else.'

His deep, exotically accented voice carried total conviction, Maddie recognized. A long-held conviction springing from his own childhood when he'd had precious little love and affection after the deaths of his parents when he was little more than a baby.

Her mouth ran dry as her heart picked up speed. He was genuinely as pleased as punch at the prospect of fatherhood. Surely he wouldn't contemplate giving any child of his into the care of a woman who plain didn't like children and wouldn't give the child the love he claimed was more important than anything?

Her head spinning with what her heart was telling her, she found herself looking up into his riveting, fantastic golden eyes as he shifted slightly and cupped her face in large, gentle hands.

For better or for worse. Logically, that was what she was accepting. Give him the children they both wanted and their marriage would remain important to him, *she* would be important to him.

And Irini? Well, as sure as night followed day Maddie couldn't see her hanging around while she, Maddie, produced gorgeous babies in the image of their charismatic father.

He loved the other woman—she herself had actually heard him express that emotion, so no way could she pretend it wasn't the case—and according to Amanda their names had been coupled, eventual marriage between them the general expectation, long before she, Maddie, had come on the scene.

Could she live with him, bear his children, knowing he still wanted the Greek woman, still loved her?

She could if she tried with everything in her to earn his love for herself. As the mother of his children she could make him forget the other woman, she answered herself, with the kind of elated determination she hadn't experienced for ages.

Feeling hypnotised by the warmth of those glinting, tawny lights, she felt her own eyes widen as her breathing fractured, the familiar tightening, the pooling of heat that surged to electrifying excitement swamping her as he murmured, 'Do we make tracks? Or do we spoil ourselves and make love again?'

'What do you think?' Her smile was luminous. Slim

arms reached for him as unstoppable response rocked through her. She simply couldn't stop loving him, wanting him, needing him. She might be stupid, walking into a trap with her eyes wide open, but this last week had taught her that she just couldn't help herself and that the trap, if there was one, could be rendered harmless by the strength of her love for him.

Even in the gathering twilight those thickly fringed eyes gleamed with molten gold as Dimitri offered, 'I forgot to ask—was your mother half as delighted as I was when you told her our news?'

Gathering her thoughts, Maddie forked up a morsel of the tender lamb in a delicious herby sauce Xanthe had prepared for the evening meal. The stone-paved terrace was lit with lanterns, and between them a candle in an amber glass bowl cast a warm glow over the delicate cast-iron table, set with dishes of salads and tiny almond cakes.

Reaching for her glass of iced water, Maddie let her eyes drift over his impressive frame. He was wearing a white shirt in the softest of cottons, tucked into a pair of narrow-fitting beat-up denim jeans, his dark hair just slightly rumpled, the evidence of emerging dark stubble shadowing his tough jawline.

In Athens he was never less than perfectly groomed, dressed in beautifully tailored dove-grey or light tan suits over pristine, exquisite shirts, and he could look intimidating. But here, like this, though still just as shatteringly handsome, he seemed warmer, wonderfully approachable.

Easy to talk to. 'I did get round to mentioning it—although I almost didn't,' she confessed, laying down her fork with a small sigh of repletion, listening to the soothing sound of the whisper of the sea as it caressed the shore far below, feeling more relaxed and at peace than she had felt in ages. 'I was too busy listening to her telling me how you bought the farm and put the deeds in their names. Why didn't you tell me?' she probed gently.

His own fork abandoned, Dimitri leant back, his features shadowed now. 'I thought you already knew— that your parents would have told you.'

Then, rough-edged, showing the first sign of discomfiture Maddie had ever seen in him, he leant forward again, fisting his hands on the top of the table, the gleam from the candle picking blue lights from his rumpled raven hair, and admitted, 'That's not true. I allowed you to believe that your parents' security depended solely on your agreement to come back to me, stay with me. When the truth is that I would have helped them regardless, because I like them and saw the injustice of what cold, big-business brains could do to small, good people with no possible means of self-defence.'

Helplessly in love with him, Maddie felt her heart twist behind her breast. Behind the tough business tycoon façade beat the generous heart of a truly good guy—a guy who would always put his family first and, in time, learn to stop loving Irini and begin to love her instead. At least that was what she was now determined on. It might take some time, but it would be worth waiting for.

Her heart melted further, until she thought that poor organ must resemble a pool of hot treacle, when he castigated, 'What I did was dishonourable! I threatened you, let that threat lie between us as the only way I could think of to make you come back to me! It was a despicable thing to do. So—'

Steeling himself, doing his best to appear to be relaxed over what in all honour had to be said, Dimitri leaned back in his seat again. For the first time in his adult life he was losing control, giving control over his happiness to another. Knowing it was what honour demanded didn't make it any easier.

'So the threat no longer exists,' he intoned heavily. 'It never did. You are free to make your own decisions about our marriage. You wanted to divorce me,' he reminded her with a studied calm that almost killed him in its achievement. 'If your reasons for wanting to end our marriage still exist—' a sudden, involuntary downward slash of one strongly crafted hand betrayed the inner tension he was trying to hide '—and whatever they are or were, I do not want to hear them, then you are free to do as you think fit.' He breathed in deeply, then stipulated forcefully, 'However, I would demand that you remain in Greece, that I have full visiting rights where our child is concerned.'

Silence hung, thick and spiky with expectation. Maddie's eyes were liquid sapphire, drenched with understanding. And awe.

This gorgeous man must have wanted her to return and take her place as his wife really badly for him to have done what he had himself named despicable and dishonourable. And it would have taken guts for him to come straight out and admit that the threats had never been real, to let it be known that the tough exterior hid a marshmallow centre.

It hadn't been about forcing her back to get her

pregnant and then rob her of her child. She knew that now. She was expecting their first baby, and already he was talking about having more children. With her. All this talk of freeing her to sue for divorce if she still wanted to was just his way of satisfying what he saw as his honour!

Happiness bubbled up inside her like a hot spring. Their future could be good. *Would* be good, she mentally emphasized. Because, on the evidence, maybe he'd already started to forget Irini and begun to fall a little in love with her before she'd left him and asked for a divorce. And he had to have been desperate for that not to happen, otherwise he wouldn't have compromised his so-valued honour and lied—in an oblique sort of way—about her parents being homeless if she dug her heels in and went for that divorce.

'Well?'

His voice was flat, but Maddie, attuned to every single thing about him, detected the underlying tension. She had kept the poor darling in suspense for far too long. Patience, as she well knew, wasn't a virtue that came easily to him.

She reached for his hand, felt his immediate response as he tightened his fingers around hers.

'Like you, I think children need both parents around on a regular basis,' she told him, with only the slightest emotional wobble in her voice she was pleased to note. 'So we stay married.'

She would be making a crucial mistake if she were to follow the impetuous need to fling herself at him and tell him she loved him to death, and that it would take a bulldozer to prise her away from him.

It was too early in their new relationship to load that onto him. He was still having to deal with his strong feelings for Irini, and if, as everything she had seen with her own eyes and heard with her own ears pointed to, they had been in love, and lovers, for ages, then at the moment that was enough for him to contend with.

He was having to face the fact that his love for the other woman was doomed. That his unsuitable wife was already pregnant. That because of his sense of what was right he could no longer contemplate handing over a large part of the coming child's care into the hands of a woman he had admitted possessed not a single maternal bone in her svelte and sexy body.

Maddie, fiddling with the stem of her glass, could only suppose that his passion for the other woman had so clouded his judgement that he had agreed to the cruel plan in the first place as being the only way out of the impasse.

And that his deep passion for another woman was something she was going to have to deal with in private if their marriage had any hope of succeeding. It was something that savaged her every time she thought about it and had to acknowledge that she was a very poor second best in his estimation.

Suddenly conscious of his silence, the quality of his concern-filled golden eyes, the tension stamped on his taut bone structure, she knew he was waiting for some-thing more—some further assurance that she had changed her mind about leaving him and was now content to settle for being the mother of his children. She knew she had to lighten the atmosphere.

So, finding a teasing tone, she released the hand that still lay in his, ran the tips of her fingers across the slash of his rigid cheekbones and down to the corner of his sensual mouth, and told him, 'And, apart from the good parents bit, the sex is out of this world!' Inwardly she quailed at the lightness and sheer shallowness of that remark when she loved him so much it actually hurt, but she forced a smile, managed a tiny shrug. 'Why would I deprive myself of it?'

CHAPTER ELEVEN

ATHENS still sweltered in the late summer heat. It was pointless wishing he and Maddie were still on the island, safe and secluded. It smacked of cowardice, a head-in-sand syndrome, and that went against all he was!

But he couldn't rid himself of the feeling that there was tension in the air, because he could sense it—an unwelcome and unprecedented feeling that something catastrophic was about to happen.

Dimitri closed the door to his aunt's quarters behind him, and fought to control both his unease and his anger.

His father's sister had been back home for three days, and each of those days had been peppered with increasingly petulant demands to know where Irini was.

'I haven't heard from her in weeks. I expected her to come and welcome me home!' had been her latest complaint. 'She's not answering her mobile phone, and that's most unlike her,' she'd fretted. 'If her parents know where she is, they're not saying. I can't imagine what the big secret is! If anyone knows, you do! I know just how close the two of you are and always will be, despite your marrying a girl who's little better than a peasant, with her eyes on your fortune!'

A man would have felt the full force of his fist at that, and known what it felt like to be flattened against the nearest wall!

As it was, his bitten out, 'If I ever hear you say one word against my wife again, or learn that you've spoken unpleasantly to her, then I shall forget the duty I owe you and ask you to leave my home,' had had to suffice.

Now he made a conscious effort to relax his rigid shoulders, unclench his teeth, calm down, and stride through the relative coolness of the house looking for Maddie. Not finding her, he bellowed to his house-keeper for information on where his wife was hiding.

He wouldn't have admitted it to a living soul, but leaving her, even for an hour or two, left him feeling wired-up, unable to forget that day—such an ordinary day, or so he'd thought—when he'd returned and dis-covered she'd left him.

Today, a crucial early-morning business meeting had necessitated his absence, and Alexandra had waylaid him on his return. And infuriated him!

He wasn't a fool. He could put two and two together as well as the next man. Since his aunt's return from Switzerland a subtle change had come over Maddie. She was strangely subdued, even with him, and that worried him. And in his aunt's presence, especially at shared mealtimes, she seemed to shrink into herself, as if trying to make herself invisible.

Couple that with the way she had seemed similarly subdued and withdrawn during the few weeks prior to the time when she'd shocked him rigid by demanding a divorce, and it didn't take a genius to work out that his aunt had been throwing a few poisoned darts in her direction!

Time to sort it out!

No one would get away with upsetting his wife while he had breath in his body!

On the arrival of the stout personage of his long-time housekeeper, he learned that Kyria Kouvaris was in the garden. He huffed out a long sigh of relief, mentally chiding himself for doubting her, for fearing that she might have broken her promise to stay with him, make their marriage work.

He who had feared nothing in the whole of his life, believing whole-heartedly that he could bend any circumstance to his will, overcome anything that life threw at him, had discovered his Achilles' heel!

She was reclining on a lounger beneath the shade of the vine arbour, a pristine folder held loosely in her hands, her eyes closed.

For a moment he allowed himself the sheer luxury of feasting his eyes on her. She wore a filmy sundress in a cool cream colour that drew attention to the honey-gold tan she had acquired on the island, the tiny shoe-string straps revealing the smooth perfection of her arms and shoulders, the soft fabric of the dress moulding those beautifully formed breasts, skimming her waist and flowing around her lovely legs.

You had to look very hard to detect the swelling of her tummy—something he allowed himself to do at leisure each time he stripped her willing body.

Abruptly he pulled himself together, his long mouth twisting wryly. He only had to see her to want her, and now was not the time!

He moved towards her. She felt his presence, turned

her head and smiled radiantly for him. 'You're back. Good! Come and see what we've got!'

Shifting into a sitting position, she moved her legs to one side, making room for him to perch on the end of the soft lounger.

Her eyes gleaming with pleasure, Maddie opened the classily presented folder. 'Look. It was delivered by hand this morning.' Spreading the enclosed papers around them, she revealed detailed sketches of the nursery Dimitri had commissioned from the team of top-flight designers he'd chosen with such care. 'It looks perfect. I love the colour scheme—pale lemon-yellow, off-white, and touches of that misty green—perfect for a baby boy or girl. And will you just look at that rocking horse? Should we give them the go-ahead to start work?'

'Of course.' Her delight was infectious. So easy to let himself get caught up in it, in the more than welcome return of the sunny smiles and easy chatter that had been markedly absent for the last few days.

But.

He collected the sketches and replaced them in the folder, then took her hands in his, his eyes serious, holding hers. 'Maddie, we'll look at them together later. Right now, I want you to tell me the truth. Has Aunt Alexandra said or done anything to upset you? Something's taken the spring out of your step since she returned. I know from experience that she has a vicious tongue when she feels like using it. And I promise you, if she has upset you and continues to do so, she will be asked to live elsewhere.'

Maddie's body clenched to stillness and her eyes smartly evaded his.

The truth? How could she?

Her joy in the morning fled. Gone was the snatched tranquillity out here, away from his aunt and the hurtful remarks the old lady had made on finding her breakfasting alone. The relaxation of the soft lounger in the welcome shade, the excitement over the plans for the nursery that had helped push the latest insult to the back of her mind faded.

'So you've got yourself pregnant? No doubt you're pleased with yourself for cementing your position as the wife of one of the wealthiest men in Greece! Well, don't make too many plans for a long-term future—I know my nephew better than you do. It won't last. He'll see through you and you'll be history!'

How could she tell him that his aunt hated her and lost no opportunity of letting her know it? The old lady had brought him up—probably done the best her intrinsically cold nature had let her, and looked on him as if he were her own son.

She couldn't in all conscience cause a family rift. And how would the old lady feel about being thrown out of the home that had been hers for so many years?

Much as she would prefer Aunt Alexandra's absence to her presence, she couldn't do it!

Conscious of his watchful silence, the increased pressure of his hands, she lifted her eyes to his and told him, trying to smile, 'There's no question of your aunt losing her home here with you. She'd be dreadfully hurt, so you mustn't even think of it! I'm a bit of a disappointment to her, that's all.' She shrugged, aiming to portray the subject's lack of importance. 'And it's understandable if you think about it, because, reading between the lines, I guess she secretly had her heart set on you marrying Irini. She's bound to be miffed because that didn't happen. Give her time and she'll get over it.'

That was as far as she could go. And if it caused him pain with the reminder that he had loved Irini for years but felt unable to marry her because of her infertility, she regretted it.

That rang true, Dimitri conceded heavily. Alexandra had doted on Irini since the day she was born, and *had* wanted to see her in Maddie's place. She probably did look on his poor darling as a usurper. But, 'There's more? Has she actually come out and said she finds you unwelcome?'

'No.'

It was horrible to lie to him. But the truth would hurt both him and his aunt. And for what? The relief of ridding herself of the old lady's insults and snide remarks? Seeing her banished would hang heavily on her conscience. Too great a cost.

It was time, more than time, that she stood her ground and refused to let Alexandra Kouvaris make her feel worse than worthless.

She found a reassuring tone. 'I guess your aunt doesn't make friends easily, but she'll come round after our baby's born—you'll see!' And if she didn't she would learn to live with it, ignore it.

'You're sure?'

Her eyes slid from his again, he noted. Her affirmative nod was ready. Too ready?

Releasing her hands, Dimitri stood. His shoulders tensed beneath the fine fabric of his smoothly tailored business suit. One of the first things that had drawn him to Maddie was her transparency. Hiding her emotions didn't come easily to her.

She was hiding something now. Something wild horses wouldn't drag from her.

But loving patience might?

Right now patience was a virtue he was struggling to achieve. He said, as evenly as he could, 'It's time for lunch. Bring the folder. We'll look at the plans in detail together.'

Misery engulfing her, Maddie swung her sandalled feet to the ground, gathering the folder of sketches and colour swatches that had earlier so delighted her.

He had sounded so flat. He was going away from her, distancing himself. Deep in the stark reminder of his lost true love?

Telling herself that she was going to have to live with the knowledge that she was second best, pretend she didn't know that savagely cutting fact for the sake of their long-term future, waiting for the gift she so longed for—the precious gift of his eventual love—she walked to where he was waiting for her.

Maddie jolted awake, naked beneath the thin cotton sheet. The house was silent as evening approached. Dimitri was no doubt still in his study, concentrating on the raft of paperwork that needed his attention—a fact he'd imparted when after lunch she'd pleaded a sudden and very real weariness and come up to their room to rest.

She had slept the whole afternoon away. Was sleep an escape mechanism? she pondered wryly, remembering how she been itching to get away from the lunch table. Away from the atmosphere.

Dimitri had been distant, as if he were lost in thought, and his aunt censorious when she, Maddie, had made the first approach of conciliation after their run-in earlier, determined not to act like a wimp and let herself be walked all over.

Passing the folder over to the old lady, she'd found a smile. 'These are the designs for the new nursery. What do you think? We'd value your opinion.'

Ignoring the folder—and the tentative peace offering—Alexandra had replied repressively, 'One doesn't read at meal-times. Besides, my opinion is unnecessary. My nephew wouldn't dream of using a designer who did not cater to his impeccable taste.'

Another put-down.

Maddie had left the room, left them to it, the atmosphere brittle.

Swinging her feet to the floor now, she noted that her slight headache had been joined by a dull ache in the small of her back. She ignored both and headed for the *en suite* bathroom and a quick shower. She would freshen up, find something pretty to wear from the lavish wardrobe Dimitri had provided after that party of unfond memory when she'd first come to Athens as his bride.

She would find Dimitri and sparkle. Coax him out of that distant mood—if he was still in it! She had recently discovered that he liked her chatter. That, according to him, she could charm the birds from the trees with it!

Did Irini babble on about this, that and everything else? Or were their private conversations more serious, more intense, centring on their love for each other? The possibility of their marrying was now never to happen, because Dimitri had gritted his teeth and settled for second best for the sake of the family he was creating, his belated sense of honour making him discard their original plans.

And because the sex was good. More than good. Though he wouldn't confide *that* slice of information to Irini!

Furious with herself for her unacceptable bout of morbid introspection, she dragged the door of the hanging cupboard open and pulled out the first garment her hand encountered. A silk shift, the colour of cornflowers. Dimitri had said it matched the colour of her eyes.

Surely he was beginning to love her just a little? Or at the least feel fondness?

It wasn't too much to hope for, was it? Because it certainly felt that way. As if he meant to play a full and dedicated part in their marriage's fresh start.

As if he was now putting her needs and happiness first, relegating Irini and his love for her to the past. So, okay, he had gone all quiet and distant on her when what she'd said had forcibly reminded him of the love he had put away from him. That was to be expected. It was early days yet, and he was to be excused because he had done the right thing, decided to make their marriage work for the sake of their coming child. Talked of their having more children in the years to come.

Promising herself that she had to believe that, she brushed her hair until it fell in soft, silky curls and tendrils around her face, applied the minimum of make-up, and set out to run him to earth.

But he seemed to be missing. The house was silent, the atmosphere heavy, as if a storm were about to break. Maddie felt perspiration on her upper lip, between her breasts. The aggravating dull ache in the small of her back seemed to be getting more intense. She must have slept in a awkward position. Strained a muscle.

When Dimitri turned up she would suggest they eat out tonight—anything to get away, to be alone with him, out of reach of the woman who always made her feel so worthless.

Yet…

Running away from a problem wasn't her style. Or it had never used to be. Only since coming here as Dimitri's bride. Irini's poisonous revelations, the way his aunt lost no opportunity to drum the fact of her nephew's enormous wealth and high social standing down her throat, contrasting it with her own lowly status, the fact that she wasn't fit to touch the ground he walked on, had turned her into a cringing wimp!

Time to sort it out! Ignoring a sudden gripping sensation in her pelvis, she headed over the main hall, making for the door that led to Alexandra's quarters. She was determined to tell the old lady that the put-downs had to stop, to suggest they try to be friends. And if she couldn't manage that, then politeness and respect would do.

Her legs felt unaccountably heavy, slowing her progress, but through the open main door she glimpsed Dimitri, jeans and T-shirt-clad, approaching along the wide driveway. He must have been for one of the long walks he was so fond of.

About to put a spurt on, let herself into his aunt's quarters before he reached the house, because for the sake of family peace the conversation she was intent on having had to be completely private, she frowned in annoyance as the telephone on a rosewood hall table shrilled out imperatively.

She couldn't simply ignore it, she decided frustratedly. But there would be other opportunities to confront the old lady, she told herself as she lifted the receiver and gave her name.

'Oh—it's you! I need to speak to Dimitri. *Now!* Fetch him!'

Irini!

She sounded hysterical. Maddie's heart went into overdrive, constricting her breathing.

'I can give him a message,' she managed, more or less evenly. Had Dimitri broken the news that he was going to stick with his marriage? Was that why the other woman sounded so manic?

A series of what sounded like curses in her own language almost split Maddie's eardrum, then, on a wild crow of spite, 'I phoned Alexandra this afternoon. She tells me you're pregnant. So don't come the high and mighty with me! The moment you've given birth you'll be yesterday's wife—I warned you, remember?'

Speechless, Maddie felt the colour drain from her face. Was he *still* putting his love for Irini first? It couldn't be true. She wouldn't let it be true!

Aware for the first time of Dimitri's presence at her side, his questioning frown, she handed him the receiver and sagged back against the wall, fighting a tide of nausea as she heard him say tersely, 'Where are you calling from? Here in Athens?' He fell silent, listening intently to what the other woman was saying, those wide shoulders tensing. Then, 'I'll be with you in fifteen minutes. Do nothing. Promise me? Let me hear you say it!'

Her breathing shallow and fast, her skin turning clammy, Maddie struggled to come to terms with what she had heard. Irini had called, and as ever he would drop everything to go to her, be with her. The undeniable fact dealt her a body-blow, left her in mind-numbing shock.

The pain around her pelvis stabbed wickedly, and white-hot horror engulfed her at that precise moment. Was she about to lose her precious baby? It mustn't happen! She wouldn't let it!

Opening her mouth to alert him to the alarming possibility, she closed it again as he turned to her, his voice sounding as if it were in an echo chamber. 'I'm sorry, but I have to go. Don't wait dinner for me.'

He mustn't! She needed him! But he was already turning towards the open doorway again. Maddie blurted the first thing to come into her head. 'Don't go—I need you!' Panic accelerated her heartbeat. He must put her first, he *must*!

But he turned back to face her, and she was sure he wasn't actually seeing her. He couldn't wait to leave. 'I have to. Irini needs me. She's threatening—' He caught the words back between his teeth. 'One day I'll tell you why, I promise. But not now. I don't have time for this. I'm sorry.'

That did it. Cleared her brain. When Irini called he had no time for his wife. Ice-cold now, her mind crystal-clear, she stated, 'Leave now and I'll take the other option you mentioned. I'll leave this marriage.' And she meant it, even though she felt her knees might buckle beneath her at any moment.

While there had been hope that they had a chance of finding happiness together she had been willing to do everything in her power to make it happen. But she would *not* be second best to that hateful woman for the rest of her days!

Dimitri went still. 'I don't accept ultimatums. Know that about me. I made a promise. I'm not about to break it.'

The ice in his tone chilled her to the depths of her being, and then he lobbed over his shoulder, already walking away from her, 'If you can make such childish threats then our marriage can't count for much, can it? Think about it. We'll talk later.'

Her brain buzzed and fizzed with dizziness, and blackness claimed her just after she watched him walk out through the door.

CHAPTER TWELVE

DIMITRI left Maddie's gynaecologist with a terse word of thanks and strode out of his office, where he'd been given a reassuring update on her condition, and along the length of the wide hospital corridor to the private room where Maddie had been for the last two days.

Hating him? Lying there, frightened for their baby, fuming because he hadn't been at her side?

Or planning to carry out her threat to walk away from their marriage as soon as she was back on her feet?

He would never understand what went on inside her head! Until that ultimatum she'd thrown at him—in an inexplicable fit of pique, or so he had supposed at the time—everything had been more than fine between them as far as he knew.

As far as he knew!

His jaw clenched. The hidden thing! Her untold initial reason for asking for a divorce.

He had categorically refused to hear her tell him those reasons. Stubbornly not wanting to know, and just as stubbornly believing that he had no need to know something that might be a constant source of distaste and sorrow in the new start he had determined they embark upon.

Something on the lines of a greedy plan to gain her freedom and take him to the cleaners at the same time? A scenario his aunt had immediately hit on, and one that he, albeit reluctantly, had almost accepted, unable to see any other.

He hadn't wanted to know, had hated the thought of having to accept that the woman he adored saw him as little more than a gold-plated meal ticket.

Head in sand, or what?

His fault!

And now that she was again threatening to end their marriage, *it,* whatever it was, had to be forced out into the open.

At least she hadn't lost the baby. And, according to her doctor, provided she took things easily for the next two or three weeks, the remainder of her pregnancy should proceed without a hitch.

And come hell or high water he'd be around to make sure she and the baby were fine.

His lean, strong features grim, he paused as he approached the room she had been given, ran his fingers through his already rumpled hair, over his stubble-roughened chin, and mentally cursed Irini and her problems. Problems she'd landed on *him*, gaining his reluctant promise to tell no one else, hysterically vowing that the only way she'd agree to taking the professional help she so obviously needed was on hearing his promise that no one else should hear about it.

It had been young Eleni who had found Maddie crumpled on the floor two days ago, who'd rushed to alert the housekeeper, who had then had the presence of mind to phone for an ambulance.

Two days. Forty-eight long hours while his Maddie had suffered. Waiting, alone, in a fever of anxiety through a whole slew of tests to discover if the tiny life inside her was safe.

Two unforgivable days since his aunt had seen fit to stir herself, lift a phone to reach his mobile and tell him of the emergency!

Two days while he'd been pandering to the needy Irini, convincing her that life *was* worth living, that her threatened overdose was foolish talk, eventually persuading her that at long last her parents must be told of the drug problem she had vowed was sorted.

Had he had the slightest idea that his Maddie was in danger of losing their baby he would not have answered Irini's hysterical call for the help she'd always insisted he alone could give her.

His teeth clenched until his jaw ached.

Had he known what he knew now the wretched woman would have been left to sort her own problems out. But at the time—to his own deep shame—he had put what he had mentally named Maddie's tantrum down to her mysterious jealousy of the other woman.

Cursing himself to hell and back, he dragged in a deep breath, expelled it slowly, relaxed his tautly held shoulders and opened the door.

Propped up against the pillows, Maddie had another stab at concentrating on the magazine one of the nurses had given her to look at. But she still felt a little drowsy from the mild sedative she'd been given yesterday, to help her relax, and the magazine—Greek language, but glamorous fashion shots—couldn't hold her interest.

Besides, she couldn't imagine herself ever trying to shoehorn herself and what she'd always considered to be her over-generous curves into any of the skinny garments so enticingly displayed. They all seemed to be designed to be worn by the models pictured—walking skeletons! Women like Irini!

Despite her earlier good intentions, tears scalded her eyes. Dimitri hadn't even bothered to phone her and see how she was doing, let alone visit. Too bound up with that dreadful woman to give a single thought to his second best wife. Had it come down to this? That Irini was even more important to him than the fate of their baby? It certainly looked like it!

A lump the size of a house brick formed in her throat. She swallowed it angrily and scrubbed at her eyes with a corner of the cotton sheet.

Enough!

What had she promised herself?

That he wasn't worth a single tear and Irini wasn't worth so much as a glancing thought. That she would think about only really positive things. Her hand moved to rest gently on her tummy. Her baby was safe. Nothing else mattered.

Certainly not a low-life like her husband, with his sordid obsession with a stick insect!

As soon as she felt able she would take the second option he'd offered back on the island. Leave him. But she would return to England, pass the waiting time at her parents' new home, where her mother would pamper her and love her. And understand.

No way would she agree to his stipulation that she stay in Greece to enable him to have frequent and ongoing access to his child. Seeing him often would keep raw wounds open and bleeding. She wouldn't do it. It would have to be a clean and total break.

By flying to Irini's side when she, his wife, had pleaded with him to stay with her, he had forfeited any rights.

And if he decided to take her to court to challenge her right to custody she'd fight him down to the last breath in her body!

Oh, for pity's sake, calm down! she told herself. Getting in a state over an unworthy slimeball would do nothing but harm. Sinking back against the pillows, she closed her eyes and tried to visualise peaceful things, like gentle waves lapping on a soft shoreline, or tranquil woodland carpeted with bluebells that swayed in an early May breeze.

But all she could see was his face!

When she heard the door open she opened her eyes, expecting to encounter a nurse, come to take her blood pressure. Again. And opened them wider when she saw the real thing, not the image that seemed indelibly printed on her retina.

Had she had a missile heavier than a mere magazine she would have thrown it at his head! As it was, she had to be content with muttering fiercely, 'Go away!'

Dimitri had to summon all his reserves of self-control to stop himself striding over to her and enfolding her in arms that ached to do just that. Hold her close and never let her go.

She had every right to be angry. But she was over-wrought, and it was imperative that she stay calm. There were dark smudges beneath the blue brilliance of her eyes, and a new fragility marked her delicate skin. His throat tightened as his hands made fists at his sides.

'You have every right to be angry,' he verbalised, his voice steady, much against his expectations. 'I only learned of what had happened half an hour or so ago, when Aunt Alexandra decided she could be bothered to contact me. I have informed her that she has to make other living arrangements before the end of the month, if not sooner. Like today!'

Maddie's fingers clutched at the edges of the sheet. She met the golden glitter of his eyes with icy determination. 'That won't be necessary,' she said flatly. 'Since there's no need to pussyfoot around now, I can tell you the truth. Your aunt's hated and despised me since she first met me. But I won't be around for her to be less than kind to, will I? Our marriage is over—remember?'

Not while he had breath in his body! Dimitri bit back that slice of information. For the next two or three weeks Maddie had to be soothed, not rendered over-emotional through arguments and recriminations.

Schooling his hard features into a mask that verged on indifference, he reminded her, 'Nevertheless, I insist you return with me—home—where you can be guaranteed peace and quiet for the baby's sake. Just until you regain your strength and we know there will be no further problems.'

And while that was happening, while he saw she was wrapped in cotton wool, was pampered, treated as if she were made of the most delicate spun glass, he would get to the bottom of the unholy mess they seemed to have created between them.

'I have spoken to your doctor and he is sure everything will be fine now—provided you take things easily for the next few weeks. That I can guarantee. You are to be discharged this evening into my care. I will collect you at six,' he added, with measured cool.

He turned then, congratulating himself that he had handled that without even a hint of an emotion that might have set her off into a frenzy of telling him that she would go nowhere with him because their marriage was dead as a dodo.

But there was little joy in that achievement, and not even the sternest self-lecture could stop him turning back at the door, his voice riven with painful regret as he announced, 'Had I had the slightest idea that a miscarriage threatened I would have told Irini in no uncertain terms to sort her own problems out. I would not have left your side for one moment!'

She had done the right thing for her unborn child, Maddie assured herself for the umpteenth time. Not for her own sake, because seeing him, being around him, nearly tore her in two.

But haring back to England the moment she was discharged from hospital would have been an irresponsible thing to do the way things were. Hadn't she been told by the best gynaecologist money could buy that she needed regular check-ups, but most of all, rest and tranquillity?

She was getting rest in spades. But tranquillity?

For the last two weeks she'd been doing her best to achieve that enviable state.

Dimitri, too, seemed to be doing his best in that regard, she acknowledged, with a dismaying lack of satisfaction.

On her return from hospital he had flatly relayed the news that his aunt was now living with Irini's parents while she looked for a suitable apartment in town and engaged a companion. Other than that there had been nothing personal, nothing that touched on their past or their future.

She saw very little of him. He appeared briefly each morning while she breakfasted, to politely ask how she was feeling. Then again at the evening meal, which they shared, imparting snippets of general information—innocuous stuff, mostly, about his friends and business colleagues, which went in one ear and out of the other because, inevitably, she itched to discuss the future, to get her life sorted, fix the date of her departure for England.

But he had made sure that didn't happen, and she knew why. He was anxious for their baby. And all that talk of making their marriage work, the future children they might have together, had to have been a con trick to make her feel secure enough to stay with him until the birth, when he would have put his cruel plan into action.

The coming child and Irini came first with him, and always would. She was simply a disposable and distant second. He had said he wouldn't have dropped everything to be with that wretched woman, had he had the benefit of hindsight, but she wasn't about to believe that. When Irini called he would go, no matter what! Otherwise he would do anything, say anything, to make sure Maddie didn't get in a state of agitation and thereby, in his mind, threaten the wellbeing of their baby.

As if she could help it!

Because although she saw so little of him, was stuck

in an uncomfortable limbo, his hand was everywhere—
and it churned her up!

There in the parcel of English novels by her favourite authors which had appeared as if by magic, in the
gorgeous bouquets of flowers that graced the suite they
had once shared, the bowls of fresh fruit and posies of
blossoms that found their way to wherever in the house
or gardens she opted to settle.

This morning, restless, she had walked the perime-
ter of the huge grounds. The weather was pleasantly
cooler now, and the emphatic expert opinion, after her
latest check-up the day before, was that everything was
going along just fine, absolutely as it should. She was
to get on with her life as normal. That made her unaccountably edgy. Almost as if she didn't want to leave
him. When she knew darn well she did!

What had been totally unexpected had been Dimitri's
reaction to the welcome news. He had stared at the
doctor as if hearing something deeply unpalatable, his
features assuming a chilling distance, and he had barely
exchanged a word with her on the drive home, engrossed in private thoughts. And last night he hadn't
dined with her as usual. The housekeeper had imparted
the information that he had been unavoidably detained
and that she wasn't to wait for him.

So what? She shrugged slim shoulders in an effort to
put him right out of her mind as she came full circle,
back to the terrace. She had the all-clear. There was now
nothing to stop her leaving, making flight arrangements
to take her back to England and away from him, making
a new life for herself and her baby, leaving him to his
obsessive passion for the stick insect!

Opting to rest on one of the loungers instead of going inside the house, she closed her eyes and waited for the inevitable.

Eleni with her tray! No doubt the staff had instructions to keep an eye on her. One of the gardeners would have relayed the information that she was back at base! Dimitri's orders, naturally. He wouldn't want her doing a disappearing act with her precious cargo.

Hearing footfalls, Maddie let her mouth curve in a smile. She had grown fond of the young Greek girl, and they had tentatively begun teaching each other their own languages. It could be hilarious, and provided a more than welcome respite from her tangled emotions where Dimitri was concerned.

Turning her head in the young girl's direction, Maddie opened her eyes—and her heart bumped to a standstill, then thundered on.

Him!

She never laid eyes on him between breakfast and the evening meal. And not always then. And now, as ever, his stupendous sexiness set off a totally unwanted leap of sensation deep in her pelvis, almost pulverising her with longing.

Hoisting herself up on her elbows, all thoughts of relaxation flying, she watched as he put a tray on a small glass-topped table within easy reach.

Coffee, for two, a plate of the little sweet cakes that were so delicious she was developing a needing-to-be-watched passion for them, the never absent small posy of flowers, and a bowl of fresh fruit.

She tensed. Speechless. Now was the perfect opportunity to put him in the picture regarding her set-in-stone decision to end their marriage. But the words wouldn't come. Her mind was in chaos.

When he sat on the end of the lounger she moved her legs sideways at the speed of light. Physical contact would make the chaos worse!

Turning to her, the force of his steely will holding her unwilling sapphire eyes, he stated flatly, 'Our child is no longer in any danger. That being the case, we have to talk. And I want the truth—the whole truth. I've been too blinkered to want to hear it. But now it's time.'

CHAPTER THIRTEEN

MADDIE'S heart leapt like a landed fish. Her hand lifted automatically to her breast, where she could feel it bumping through the fine white organza of her sleeveless top.

Why now, when everything was over between them? When she could walk away with some dignity, without laying her broken heart before him, suffering his scorn or—heaven forbid—his pity?

Yet—her brow furrowed with indecision—maybe telling him what she knew, had known for ages, would be a catharsis, a cleansing. Keeping it locked inside her, where it would fester for the rest of her life, would do her no good at all, deny her any kind of closure.

'Maddie?' he prompted. His voice was gentle. 'Tell me what made you demand a divorce all those weeks ago.'

A muscle in her throat jerked and her eyes slid away from his.

Dimitri knew he couldn't take it if she refused to give him any explanation, or told him that his suspicions had been right all along.

Whatever—he had to know why she was determined to end their marriage. 'When we agreed to make a fresh start, after we discovered you were carrying my child, I wouldn't let you tell me why you'd left me. I was wrong to insist that the slate had to be wiped clean. It was a form of cowardice and I'm not proud of that. I was desperate to keep you, to make you happy. I just wanted to start over.'

A sigh was wrenched from him before he stated, 'But the slate isn't clean, is it? Again you threaten to leave me, so the stain must still be there. So tell me. Is it money? I need to know.'

He enclosed her hand in his lean, bronzed one and his touch was fire in her veins. Maddie swung her feet to the ground and shot upright, dragging her hand from his.

She didn't need this! This instinctive reaction to his touch!

And she didn't want a pay-off. How could he think that? His wealth had never interested her. And now this demeaning physical reminder of the way he could make her feel, the agony of loving, wanting and needing him that she couldn't shake off—no matter how often and how staunchly she informed herself that she hated and despised him!

The trouble was, she knew herself too well. With him she had always found it so easy, so imperative, to give of herself, to respond. But she was not going to let herself fall into the abyss of blind love and yearning again!

She turned back to face him. He was standing now, and his tall, powerful physique gave her the feeling of being overwhelmed. Wrapping her arms self-protectively around her midriff, she met his eyes, determination in the sparkling blue.

But her mouth shook a little when she got out, 'We'd

been married for just a few days when Irini told me exactly why you'd picked me.'

'And?' His hands came down on her rigid shoulders. He looked bemused. His strongly marked brows drawn together in a slight frown of incomprehension. Her spine stiffened until she thought it might splinter.

'Big hips, humble background. No-account,' she supplied, on a hiss of breath. 'The sort of dumb-cluck who wouldn't know how to fight you when you did what you meant to do.'

'*Pethi mou—*'

'Don't!' She wrenched away from him. Empty endearments she could do without! Fat tears scalded her face. With one swift movement he captured her waist and drew her back to him.

'Irini made these insults?'

His eyes challenged her, as if he believed she was lying. Or perhaps as if he couldn't believe his lover's stupidity in showing her hand so early in the game?

'Who else?' Maddie ground out, frustrated at his pretence of not knowing what she was on about. 'And for good measure she told me the rest of it! You're madly in love with each other but can't marry because she can't give you the heir you need!'

She was almost yelling now, incensed by the hurt she'd been dealt. 'So *bingo!* You'd get yourself a no-account wife, get her pregnant, and as soon as the child was born you'd take it and dump her. Goodbye, and thanks a bunch! And, hey! Know what? You'd be able to take the wife you *really* loved and wanted! So it's no good you trying to pretend you want me for anything other than the baby!'

Suddenly the fight drained out of her. She felt limp and utterly wretched.

Her head drooped. His hands tightened about her waist as he moved her back to the lounger. 'Sit. Before you fall down.'

Those strong, lean features might have been carved out of granite, Maddie registered as she did as she'd been told—sat, because she felt weak and empty and keeping upright suddenly seemed beyond her.

'So when did this—conversation—take place?' He sank down beside her. Much too close. She was far too aware of his body heat, the signature scent of him, all male, and faintly, cleanly lemony. It was sheer torture.

What did that matter now? Numbly, she considered his question. He was obviously intent on prising every last detail from her, and she really didn't want to talk about it any more. Why didn't he just face the fact that he'd been found out? Admit it and start negotiations— involving money, of course—to try and persuade her to hand her child over willingly?

Drained, Maddie passed a hand over her forehead. The skin felt tight. He was waiting, watching her intently. 'The meet-the-bride party you threw for your friends, remember?' She answered at last with listless resignation. Even thinking about that encounter turned her stomach, and talking about it with the man who was the co-instigator of all her humiliation and misery was a thousand times worse.

'Maddie—' Lean fingers cupped her chin, forcing her to meet his eyes. Shamefully, hers misted with tears. 'Why didn't you tell me?'

He wasn't denying it, she registered with helpless

misery. Had she wanted him to? Wanted him to force her to believe him so that she could go on living in a fool's paradise for just a little longer?

Appalled by her weakness, she twisted away from him, hauled herself together and admitted tersely, 'I wish I had! I'd been out on the terrace, hiding from those of the guests who looked at me as if I were some kind of strange peasant who'd wandered into a royal gala occasion by mistake! I was on my way back in, all fired-up. I was going to ask you if it was true. But I bumped into Amanda and she told me to cool it. She said Irini was a spiteful, malicious bitch and jealous. We'd only just got married, and she said if I went in there and caused a scene it would embarrass you in front of your classy guests and make you think I didn't trust you.'

Her fingers were pleating the white organza of her floaty skirt and, her head lowered, she muttered, 'I took her advice. And then it was too late.'

'Why?' Feeling shell-shocked Dimitri knew that Maddie's well-being, the reassurance he must give her, was the only thing stopping him marching out of there, dragging Irini back by the scruff of her neck and forcing her to get down on her knees and beg his darling's for-giveness for such monstrous lies.

'None of this rubbish is true,' he hastened to tell her, desperately trying to smother the fear that it might, as she'd said, be too late, that the damage done was irrep-arable. Those telling words *too late* echoed hollowly in his brain, and he took her restless hands in his.

'Isn't it?' She answered his repudiation flatly, almost without interest, as if his denials were worthless, not worth listening to.

Her hands lay limply within his. She hadn't the energy to drag them away, simply told him, 'Your aunt lost no opportunity to remind me that I wasn't fit to touch the ground you walked on. And between that and the way Irini took all your attention when she was around, and the way you'd insisted on a dead quiet wedding, as if you were ashamed of me, I lost all my self-confidence. It all seemed to add up—and that was really awful. So I couldn't tell you what I knew, what Irini had said to me, because I wouldn't be able to hide how very much you'd hurt me. I might not have your breeding, your social clout or your hefty bank balance. But I do have some pride!'

She gave a monumentally inelegant sniff, gathered herself and reminded him shakily, 'That last morning I came down and you were speaking to Irini on the phone. You said you loved her. That you'd be with her in minutes. I knew the worst then. It wasn't just a nasty niggle at the back of my mind. So I left. And how could I tell you why?' she blurted, her eyes brimming. 'Tell you how much I was hurting because I loved you to pieces and to you I was just a means to an end?'

By that admission she'd gone and betrayed herself, she recognised agonisingly. To make up for that too-telling slice of information, she blurted, 'Then you forced me to come back to you with a lie! And went on about how many children we'd have. So, sucker-like, I swallowed it. I decided you'd put what you felt for Irini behind you and settled for me because I could give you the family you wanted, and perhaps you were even getting just a bit fond of me.'

'Just a bit—' Dimitri began, astounded, hurt by her hurt.

She snapped his words off with an anguished, 'Shut up! I knew just what a fool I'd been because you went to her when I'd pleaded with you to stay with me. You point-blank refused. You went to her. And stayed with her. For two whole days. When I needed you!'

With a heartfelt groan Dimitri ground out, 'I will never forgive myself for that, *chrysi mou!* I can only plead ignorance of the facts!' Sweeping aside any objection she might make, he lifted her in his arms and strode through the vast house as if burdened with no more than a feather, bellowing for the housekeeper, issuing to that startled personage instructions for chilled fruit juice to be brought to their suite.

'I have much to explain—my case to plead,' he imparted briskly as he closed the door to the master bedroom with an Italian-crafted-leather-shod foot. 'And you, my sweetest delight, are overwrought when you must be calm,' he stated firmly, as he tenderly laid her stunned-into-compliance form on the bed, arranged pillows behind her head and removed her shoes.

Watching the assured movements of that perfectly honed body as he strode back to the door, flung it open and just stood there, waiting, clicking his fingers with an impatience which boded no good at all for any tardiness, Maddie decided she might as well stay just where she was. She was too emotionally wrung out to dredge up the strength to do anything else.

Taking the tray, dismissing the breathless housekeeper, Dimitri carried it to the bed-table, set it down, and poured chilled fruit juice into a tall glass.

His heart clenched with the pain of all that bitch had put Maddie through. The reason he'd misguidedly attributed to her desire to leave their marriage was contemptibly way off the mark.

She was lying where he'd left her, her soft mouth still mutinous. But her huge eyes were lost, haunted and hollow, the tissue-thin skin stretched tightly over her cheekbones, strain showing in her pallor.

He swallowed around the tightness in his throat. 'Drink this.' She was slow to react, but eventually she took the glass, took a mouthful, her teeth chattering against the glass, and handed it back. Sitting beside her, he fought the instinct to take her in his arms. Too soon. He needed all the patience at his command.

'Let me explain about Irini. You overheard me say I loved her. I do. Or did. After what you've told me I think I despise her.' Briefly, his long mouth compressed. 'As a child, after the deaths of my parents, Irini was the only playmate I was allowed to have. I came to look on her as a sister. Loved her as a sister. Nothing more. As she grew into her teens she seemed to rely on me more and more. I became the recipient of all her troubles—which were, as I told her, either of her own making or in her imagination.'

His brows drew down. 'With hindsight, I should have seen the growing problem. But I didn't. Her neediness brought out a half-exasperated protectiveness in me. I looked on her as the little sister I'd never had, remember?' He sighed, touched her hand just briefly with his. 'And now I will break a promise for the first time in my life, because you, your happiness, are far more important.'

Expression flickered in the blue depths of her eyes for the first time since he'd carried her up here. The beginnings of belief in him? He hoped so.

He captured both her unresistant hands. 'Irini has a drugs and drink problem. When I discovered this, I was appalled. I made her face up to the damage she was doing to herself, persuaded her to seek professional help. I booked her into a clinic here in Greece. In return she made me swear I would tell no one. Not her parents, and certainly not Aunt Alexandra, who has always doted on her and from whom she expects to inherit a large fortune,' he added drily. 'The phone call you over-heard—well, that was a shock to me. She'd walked out of the clinic, was back in Athens and threatening to take an overdose. She was weeping, asking me if I loved her. I said I did—but as an exasperating and worrying little sister. I had no option but to try to reassure her, to go to her, persuade her to return to the clinic. I saw her into a taxi, then called into the office. I came home and you'd gone.'

'She was here when you brought me back from England. All over you like a second skin,' Maddie reminded him thinly.

Heartened by the first tangible sign that she'd been listening to a word he'd been saying, Dimitri agreed. 'So she was. And no one could have been more annoyed than I! But because of the state I knew she was in I had to treat her with kid gloves. Apparently she'd instructed the driver to bring her straight back to Athens, had arrived here and obviously heard from Aunt that you'd left me. It was what she wanted—though I had not the slightest inkling of that then. I knew something had to be settled. With her adamant hysterical refusal to let her parents know what was happening, the responsibility fell on me—even though it was the last thing I wanted or needed at that time. All I wanted, needed, was to put our marriage back on track.'

'Why?' Maddie hoisted herself up on her elbows. She felt stronger now, more alive, determined to get to the bottom of this unholy mess. His talk about Irini's problems, his brotherly love, did ring true. Yet…'For the children I could give you?'

'*Chrysi mou!*' A ferocious little frown had gathered between her crystal-clear eyes. 'That you will give me children, God willing, is a blessing. But I will still love you until the day I die if that never happens,' he assured her emotionally, leaning forward to kiss the frown away, murmuring, 'You will get wrinkles!'

'And?' she got out chokily.

'I will love them. As I will always love everything about you.'

'You've never said the love word.' Maddie could hardly speak for the fluttering of unbearable hope that coursed through her. But could she trust it?

Cupping her face between his lean hands, he had the grace to look discomfited as he confessed, 'I never got the hang of it. I don't remember if my parents told me they loved me, but I know they must have done. After that, my life was a series of chilly rules and regulations.' He shrugged. Then beamed. 'But I'm telling you now! I fell fathoms deep that first day, remember? In the courtyard. You were wearing tatty old shorts, had smears of dirt on your lovely face. And freckles! I knew I was in love for the first time in my life, and vowed I would make you my wife!'

Somehow he was on the bed beside her, holding her, but Maddie wasn't going to let herself melt into him.

Instead, she said firmly, 'Do you promise on our child's life that all that stuff Irini told me wasn't true?'

Golden eyes widened. He looked as if she had asked him to swear the earth wasn't flat. He hoisted himself up on one elbow, his mouth quirking. 'My Maddie, sometimes I think you don't possess even one streak of logic in your beautiful head!' A gentle finger made an exploratory journey over the fullness of her lower lip.

'Think about it. If she and I had indeed made such absurdly Machiavellian plans, would she have alerted you to them right at the beginning of our marriage, when it would have ruined everything? Of course not!' He answered his own question with that well-remembered supreme self-assurance. 'She would have held her tongue, done and said nothing to make you suspicious, kept her fingers crossed, and hoped you remained in ignorance!'

'Oh!' Feeling monumentally stupid for not having worked that out for herself, she felt colour wash over her face.

Contrite at having pointed out her lack in the logic department, he amended, 'I can see why you fell for it, though. You implied you were feeling out of your depth at the time. And Aunt's spitefulness would have further dented your feelings of self-worth. For which she will go unforgiven. And as for Irini—well, my only guess is she saw you as a threat to what I can now see as her possessive feelings towards me. She wanted you out of my life and used the most far-fetched and ridiculous pack of lies I have ever heard! Amanda was quite right in insisting that Irini was just a spiteful, malicious woman. But wrong in advising you not to tell me.'

'Don't I know it?' Maddie mourned with real regret. And then forgot any further explanations as he kissed her.

He lifted his handsome head long minutes later to state thickly, 'Now everything is right between us? No more misgivings, doubts, *chrysi mou?*'

Everything inside her yearned to say *Yes, of course!* But there was still that raw spot, so recent it was capable of hurt. 'So what was so important that you had to go to her a couple of weeks ago, when I asked you to stay with me?'

He stilled. She thought he wasn't going to answer. Then he shrugged, his golden eyes rueful. 'I'm sorry. I don't like to be reminded of the worst failure of my life.' He took a long breath. 'I was absent for the week before we went to the island, remember?'

Maddie nodded speechlessly. How could she forget? She'd been convinced he and Irini were together.

'I was at the end of my tether,' he confessed impatiently, as if that state of affairs was anathema to him. 'You'd told me you wanted a divorce. I was determined to make you change your mind. On top of that, in refusing necessary treatment Irini had become a constant albatross around my neck. I needed all my energy to convince you to stay with me. So I decided to get her sorted out once and for all—get her off my back. I booked her into a clinic in California and personally escorted her there, thinking she'd be in good hands and far enough away to ensure she would think twice about just walking out.'

Anger darkened his eyes. 'But that is what the wretched woman did! She was back in Athens and again threatening to kill herself. I couldn't take the risk that she didn't mean it. I wouldn't have my worst enemy's death on my conscience, never mind the woman I'd always looked on as a needy little sister. It took me two days to convince her that her problems weren't over, as she claimed, and that her suicide threats were simply a cry for help. That I could no longer provide that help and her parents had to be told.' He sighed heavily. 'Apparently Aunt Alexandra was the first person she contacted when she got back to Athens. She learned that you were expecting our baby, and I guess that tipped her over the edge.'

He cupped her face in his hands and Maddie noticed the strain etched on his tight features, the set of his sensual mouth. 'I will never be able to get within two miles of that woman without wanting to throttle her!' His voice was roughened, the sexy accent more pronounced than she had ever heard it. 'She did you great harm. Can you ever forgive me for failing you when you most needed me?'

For answer Maddie leaned into him and wound her slender arms around his neck. 'I already have!' Her smile was radiant. He loved her, and she loved him to pieces! And the feared Irini was just an irritating thorn in his side! 'You didn't know what was happening to me. It had only just dawned on me—that I might be about to miscarry, I mean.' His fantastic eyes were beginning to lose that self-condemning harshness, so she pressed on, 'You were doing the honourable thing— looking out for someone in distress. I know you'd never understood why I disliked Irini—how could you? And when I threw that panicky ultimatum at you, naturally you decided I was throwing a jealous tantrum.'

He closed both arms tightly around her and she laid

her bright head against his shoulder and murmured, 'Try not to think too harshly of Irini. Her head must have been really messed up. After our marriage she could see her prop—you—being taken away so she lashed out at me.'

That fairy story had probably been wishful thinking. Irini had been in love with Dimitri for years, hanging on to his protective concern for her for grim life, because that was all he'd ever offered, privately hoping for his love. But Maddie wouldn't offer that piece of logic. Why burden him with it when in the past he had been unable to see what was right under his nose?

'You are too generous, *chrysi mou*. Every day, every hour, I love you more and more, until I think I will explode with it!'

She could feel his heart thumping against hers. Her breathing quickened. She could afford to be generous when she had the blessing of his love. When she knew he would avoid the other woman like the plague in future. She lifted her face to his, her eyes drenched with emotion. 'I love you more than I can ever tell you,' she confessed.

His beautiful eyes were intense. 'Then our marriage is safe?'

'As the Bank of England! Please kiss me!'

So he did. He took her lips with an aching tenderness that brought tears of joy to her eyes and she wriggled closer to him and felt his body leap at the contact. The kiss deepened until she quivered with longing and just had to lie back against the pillows, making sure he came with her. In no time at all he was reverently sliding the fabric of her top away from her shoulders, until something stilled his hands and made his voice emerge on a determined tone.

'Did you really mind about having a quiet wedding? If I deprived you, then I will arrange a blessing—a fabulous designer gown, bridesmaids, flowers and bells, a zillion guests in fancy hats! Just say the word!'

Giggling at his extravagance, Maddie ran her fingers through his rumpled hair. 'I *loved* our wedding! I don't go a bundle on splashy displays. And I promise I only threw that at you because your aunt tried to use it to make me feel inferior!'

Pushing her tumbling fringe out of her eyes, he kissed her again, briefly, then held her eyes with his and said ruefully, 'If I'm honest, then I have to tell you that had I had my way we would have had a wedding to rival royalty! I wanted to show you off to the whole world! But…' His lips compressed. 'Your father is the most stubborn of men.' His sudden smile dazzled her. 'I think you inherited the pride gene from him! Imagine my dilemma when, as father of the bride, he insisted that he should pay for the wedding—every last penny. I guessed he didn't have money to throw around, so what could I do but settle for the most low-key celebration known to man and announce that that was what we wanted—much though it went against the grain?'

'Not just gorgeous, but sensitive and caring! Oh, Dimitri, I do love you!' She tipped her head to drop kisses along his tough jawline. 'Now, shut up, do! Stop tormenting me—and carry on where you left off!'

So he did. To her complete satisfaction. And his.

Maddie walked up through the gardens. Sweltering. Her knees were grubby where she'd been kneeling in the earth. Her face would be smeared with perspiration and dirt, too. But she couldn't be happier. Her work on the neglected hollow of land at the far end of the grounds had afforded her great satisfaction, and Dimitri had looked on with interest and pride as she'd transformed it into an oasis of perfumed lilies, jasmine and lavender. The loveliest of places to sit in the cool of the evening, talking, laughing and relaxing together over a shared bottle of wine.

She couldn't be happier if she tried, she reflected as, reaching the terrace, she saw her darling little Nik wriggle down from Eleni's arms and scamper towards her on his sturdy little legs.

Lifting him up, she cuddled him closely. At sixteen months old he showed definite promise of becoming the spitting image of his handsome father.

Dismissing the smiling Eleni in the Greek she had been at pains to acquire, she dropped a kiss on the end of Nik's little nose and reverted to English, 'Time for your afternoon nap, sweetheart. And Daddy will be back to play with you after tea.'

Dimitri had proved to be a very hands-on father, and her heart wriggled inside her as she thought about the news she had to give him. But telling him he was about to be a father again would wait until they were on their special island tomorrow. And this year they would be taking Nik, which would be wonderful.

Alerted, as she always was, she looked up to see Dimitri emerging into the sunlight from the cool interior of the house. Wearing an immaculate dove-grey business suit, he was handsome as all-get-out. And when he gave her that slow, sexy smile of his and remarked, 'Tatty old shorts, dirty face. And freckles,' her heart just turned to treacle.

He loved her to bits, no matter how dishevelled she looked. And tonight she would be in a completely different guise. Wearing a sleek and beautiful designer gown, jewels at her throat, her hair tamed and piled on top of her head, she would be ready to mingle with the great and the good at the glittering charity gala that marked the end of the social season before everyone who was anyone fled Athens for cooler climes.

Because Dimitri treated her like a princess her self-confidence had returned in spades, and she was comfortable in any company.

Their eyes held as he took his excited little son into his arms and told her, 'I'll settle him for his nap while you get ready to take a shower. Then I'll join you. I've got the feeling that some pretty extensive work with a soapy hand is called for.'

Meeting the devilment in those fabulous gold eyes turned her grubby knees to water, and, in a fever of excitement, it was all she could do to get up to their room, where she stripped off and felt her breasts tighten in anticipation. The liquid, wanton heat pooling between her thighs was sizzling, the sizzling intensifying a thousandfold as he walked in to join her.

His tie had been discarded, and he'd left his suit jacket somewhere, and his lean hands were already dealing with the buttons of his pristine shirt as his eyes drifted over her with possessive intent and he said, 'Serious soapy attention, indeed...'

REQUEST YOUR FREE BOOKS!

HARLEQUIN® *Presents*~®

2 FREE NOVELS PLUS 2 FREE GIFTS!

PASSION GUARANTEED SEDUCTION

YES! Please send me 2 FREE Harlequin Presents® novels and my 2 FREE gifts. After receiving them, if I don't wish to receive any more books, I can return the shipping statement marked "cancel." If I don't cancel, I will receive 6 brand-new novels every month and be billed just $3.80 per book in the U.S., or $4.47 per book in Canada, plus 25¢ shipping and handling per book and applicable taxes, if any*. That's a savings of close to 15% off the cover price! I understand that accepting the 2 free books and gifts places me under no obligation to buy anything. I can always return a shipment and cancel at any time. Even if I never buy another book from Harlequin, the two free books and gifts are mine to keep forever.

106 HDN EEXK   306 HDN EEXV

Name _____ (PLEASE PRINT)

Address _____ Apt. # _____

City _____ State/Prov. _____ Zip/Postal Code _____

Signature (if under 18, a parent or guardian must sign)

Mail to the Harlequin Reader Service®:
IN U.S.A.: P.O. Box 1867, Buffalo, NY 14240-1867
IN CANADA: P.O. Box 609, Fort Erie, Ontario L2A 5X3

Not valid to current Harlequin Presents subscribers.

Want to try two free books from another line?
Call 1-800-873-8635 or visit www.morefreebooks.com.

* Terms and prices subject to change without notice. NY residents add applicable sales tax. Canadian residents will be charged applicable provincial taxes and GST. This offer is limited to one order per household. All orders subject to approval. Credit or debit balances in a customer's account(s) may be offset by any other outstanding balance owed by or to the customer. Please allow 4 to 6 weeks for delivery.

Your Privacy: Harlequin is committed to protecting your privacy. Our Privacy Policy is available online at www.eHarlequin.com or upon request from the Reader Service. From time to time we make our lists of customers available to reputable firms who may have a product or service of interest to you. If you would prefer we not share your name and address, please check here. ☐

HP07

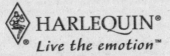

HARLEQUIN *Presents*

ITALIAN HUSBANDS

They're tall, dark...and ready to marry!

If you love reading about our sensual Italian men, don't delay.
Look out for the next story in this great miniseries.
Coming soon in Harlequin Presents!

SICILIAN HUSBAND, BLACKMAILED BRIDE
by **Kate Walker**

Dark, proud and sinfully gorgeous,
Guido Corsentino must reclaim his wife.
But Amber ran away from him once,
and Guido resolves to protect her from the
consequences of her actions...in his bed!

www.eHarlequin.com   HPIH0407

HARLEQUIN *Presents*

Proud and passionate…

Three billionaires are soon to discover
the truth to their ancestry.

*Though royalty is their destiny, these sheikhs
are as untamed as their homeland!*

The Desert Princes

**From the magnificent Blue Palace to the wild
plains of the desert, you'll be swept away as three
sheikh princes find their brides.**

THE SHEIKH'S UNWILLING WIFE
by **Sharon Kendrick**

Five years ago Alexa walked out on her sham of a
marriage, but Giovanni is determined that Alexa should
resume her position as his wife. Though how will he
react when he discovers that he has a son?

On sale April 2007